INNOCENT ERÉNDIRA AND OTHER STORIES

INNOCENT ERÉNDIRA

Translated from the Spanish by Gregory Rabassa

NEW YORK, HAGERSTOWN, SAN FRANCISCO, LONDON

1817

GABRIEL GARCÍA MÁRQUEZ

AND OTHER STORIES

HARPER & ROW, PUBLISHERS

The stories in this work were published separately in Spain. "The Incredible and Sad Tale of Innocent Eréndira and Her Heartless Grandmother" appeared in *Esquire* magazine.
Portions of "The Sea of Lost Time" appeared in *The New Yorker.*
Portions of "Death Constant Beyond Love" appeared in *The Atlantic Monthly.*
"Bitterness for Three Sleepwalkers" appeared in *Translation*.

FIRST EDITION

Designed by Sidney Feinberg

Library of Congress Cataloging in Publication Data

García Márquez, Gabriel, 1928-
  Innocent Eréndira, and other stories.
  CONTENTS: The incredible and sad tale of Innocent Eréndira and her heartless grandmother.—The sea of lost time—Death constant beyond love—The third resignation. [etc.]
  I.Title.
PZ4.G2164In   [PQ8180.7.A73]   863   74-15873
ISBN 0-06-011416-9

78 79 80 81 82 10 9 8 7 6 5 4 3 2 1

Contents

The Incredible and Sad Tale of Innocent Eréndira and Her Heartless Grandmother

Eréndira was bathing her grandmother when the wind of her misfortune began to blow. The enormous mansion of moonlike concrete lost in the solitude of the desert trembled down to its foundations with the first attack. But Eréndira and her grandmother were used to the risks of the wild nature there, and in the bathroom decorated with a series of peacocks and childish mosaics of Roman baths they scarcely paid any attention to the caliber of the wind.

The grandmother, naked and huge in the marble tub, looked like a handsome white whale. The granddaughter had just turned fourteen and was languid, soft-boned, and too meek for her age. With a parsimony that had something like sacred rigor about it, she was bathing her grandmother with water in which purifying herbs and aromatic leaves had been boiled, the latter clinging to the succulent back, the flowing metal-colored hair, and the powerful shoulders which were so mercilessly tattooed as to put sailors to shame.

"Last night I dreamt I was expecting a letter," the grandmother said.

Eréndira, who never spoke except when it was unavoidable, asked:

"What day was it in the dream?"

"Thursday."

"Then it was a letter with bad news," Eréndira said, "but it will never arrive."

When she had finished bathing her grandmother, she took her to her bedroom. The grandmother was so fat that she could only walk by leaning on her granddaughter's shoulder or on a staff that looked like a bishop's crosier, but even during her most difficult efforts the power of an antiquated grandeur was evident. In the bedroom, which had been furnished with an excessive and somewhat demented taste, like the whole house, Eréndira needed two more hours to get her grandmother ready. She untangled her hair strand by strand, perfumed and combed it, put an equatorially flowered dress on her, put talcum powder on her face, bright red lipstick on her mouth, rouge on her cheeks, musk on her eyelids, and mother-of-pearl polish on her nails, and when she had her decked out like a larger than life-size doll, she led her to an artificial garden with suffocating flowers that were like the ones on the dress, seated her in a large chair that had the foundation and the pedigree of a throne, and left her listening to elusive records on a phonograph that had a speaker like a megaphone.

While the grandmother floated through the swamps of the past, Eréndira busied herself sweeping the house, which was dark and motley, with bizarre furniture and statues of invented Caesars, chandeliers of teardrops and alabaster angels, a gilded piano, and numerous clocks of unthinkable sizes and shapes. There was a cistern in the courtyard for the storage of water carried over many years from distant springs on the backs of Indians, and hitched to a ring on the cistern wall was a broken-down ostrich, the only feathered creature who could survive the torment of that accursed climate. The house was far away from everything, in the heart of the desert, next to a settlement with miserable and burning streets where the goats committed suicide from desolation when the wind of misfortune blew.

That incomprehensible refuge had been built by the grandmother's husband, a legendary smuggler whose name was Amadís, by whom she had a son whose name was also Amadís and who was Eréndira's father. No one knew either the origins or the motivations of that family. The best known version in the language of the Indians was that Amadís the father had rescued his beautiful wife from a house of prostitution in the Antilles, where he had killed a man in a knife fight, and that he had transplanted her forever in the impunity of the desert. When the Amadíses died, one of melancholy fevers and the other riddled with bullets in a fight over a woman, the grandmother buried their bodies in the courtyard, sent away the fourteen barefoot servant girls, and continued ruminating on her dreams of grandeur in the shadows of the furtive house, thanks to the sacrifices of the bastard granddaughter whom she had reared since birth.

Eréndira needed six hours just to set and wind the clocks.

The day when her misfortune began she didn't have to do that because the clocks had enough winding left to last until the next morning, but on the other hand, she had to bathe and overdress her grandmother, scrub the floors, cook lunch, and polish the crystalware. Around eleven o'clock, when she was changing the water in the ostrich's bowl and watering the desert weeds around the twin graves of the Amadíses, she had to fight off the anger of the wind, which had become unbearable, but she didn't have the slightest feeling that it was the wind of her misfortune. At twelve o'clock she was wiping the last champagne glasses when she caught the smell of broth and had to perform the miracle of running to the kitchen without leaving a disaster of Venetian glass in her wake.

She just managed to take the pot off the stove as it was beginning to boil over. Then she put on a stew she had already prepared and took advantage of a chance to sit down and rest on a stool in the kitchen. She closed her eyes, opened them again with an unfatigued expression, and began pouring the soup into the tureen. She was working as she slept.

The grandmother had sat down alone at the head of a banquet table with silver candlesticks set for twelve people. She shook her little bell and Eréndira arrived almost immediately with the steaming tureen. As Eréndira was serving the soup, her grandmother noticed the somnambulist look and passed her hand in front of her eyes as if wiping an invisible pane of glass. The girl didn't see the hand. The grandmother followed her with her look and when Eréndira turned to go back to the kitchen, she shouted at her:

"Eréndira!"

Having been awakened all of a sudden, the girl dropped the tureen onto the rug.

"That's all right, child," the grandmother said to her with assuring tenderness. "You fell asleep while you were walking about again."

"My body has that habit," Eréndira said by way of an excuse.

Still hazy with sleep, she picked up the tureen, and tried to clean the stain on the rug.

"Leave it," her grandmother dissuaded her. "You can wash it this afternoon."

So in addition to her regular afternoon chores, Eréndira had to wash the dining room rug, and she took advantage of her presence at the washtub to do Monday's laundry as well, while the wind went around the house looking for a way in. She had so much to do that night came upon her without her realizing it, and when she put the dining room rug back in its place it was time to go to bed.

The grandmother had been fooling around on the piano all afternoon, singing the songs of her times to herself in a falsetto, and she had stains of musk and tears on her eyelids. But when she lay down on her bed in her muslin nightgown, the bitterness of fond memories returned.

"Take advantage of tomorrow to wash the living room rug too," she told Eréndira. "It hasn't seen the sun since the days of all the noise."

"Yes, Grandmother," the girl answered.

She picked up a feather fan and began to fan the implacable matron, who recited the list of nighttime orders to her as she sank into sleep.

"Iron all the clothes before you go to bed so you can

sleep with a clear conscience."

"Yes, Grandmother."

"Check the clothes closets carefully, because moths get hungrier on windy nights."

"Yes, Grandmother."

"With the time you have left, take the flowers out into the courtyard so they can get a breath of air."

"Yes, Grandmother."

"And feed the ostrich."

She had fallen asleep but she was still giving orders, for it was from her that the granddaughter had inherited the ability to be alive still while sleeping. Eréndira left the room without making any noise and did the final chores of the night, still replying to the sleeping grandmother's orders.

"Give the graves some water."

"Yes, Grandmother."

"And if the Amadíses arrive, tell them not to come in," the grandmother said, "because Porfirio Galán's gang is waiting to kill them."

Eréndira didn't answer her any more because she knew that the grandmother was getting lost in her delirium, but she didn't miss a single order. When she finished checking the window bolts and put out the last lights, she took a candlestick from the dining room and lighted her way to her bedroom as the pauses in the wind were filled with the peaceful and enormous breathing of her sleeping grandmother.

Her room was also luxurious, but not so much as her grandmother's, and it was piled high with the rag dolls and wind-up animals of her recent childhood. Overcome by the barbarous chores of the day, Eréndira didn't have the strength to get undressed and she put the candlestick on the night table and fell onto the bed. A short while later the wind of her misfortune came into the bedroom like a pack of hounds and knocked the candle over against the curtain.

At dawn, when the wind finally stopped, a few thick and scattered drops of rain began to fall, putting out the last embers and hardening the smoking ashes of the mansion. The people in the village, Indians for the most part, tried to rescue the remains of the disaster: the charred corpse of the ostrich, the frame of the gilded piano, the torso of a statue. The grandmother was contemplating the residue of her fortune with an impenetrable depression. Eréndira, sitting between the two graves of the Amadíses, had stopped weeping. When the grandmother was convinced that very few things remained intact among the ruins, she looked at her granddaughter with sincere pity.

"My poor child," she sighed. "Life won't be long enough for you to pay me back for this mishap."

She began to pay it back that very day, beneath the noise of the rain, when she was taken to the village storekeeper, a skinny and premature widower who was quite well known in the desert for the good price he paid for virginity. As the grandmother waited undauntedly, the widower examined Eréndira with scientific austerity: he considered the strength of her thighs, the size of her breasts, the diameter of her hips. He didn't say a word until he had some calculation of what she was worth.

"She's still quite immature," he said then. "She has the teats of a bitch."

Then he had her get on a scale to prove his decision with

figures. Eréndira weighed ninety pounds.

"She isn't worth more than a hundred pesos," the widower said.

The grandmother was scandalized.

"A hundred pesos for a girl who's completely new!" she almost shouted. "No, sir, that shows a great lack of respect for virtue on your part."

"I'll make it a hundred and fifty," the widower said.

"This girl caused me damages amounting to more than a million pesos," the grandmother said. "At this rate she'll need two hundred years to pay me back."

"You're lucky that the only good feature she has is her age," the widower said.

The storm threatened to knock the house down, and there were so many leaks in the roof that it was raining almost as much inside as out. The grandmother felt all alone in a world of disaster.

"Just raise it to three hundred," she said.

"Two hundred and fifty."

Finally they agreed on two hundred and twenty pesos in cash and some provisions. The grandmother then signaled Eréndira to go with the widower and he led her by the hand to the back room as if he were taking her to school.

"I'll wait for you here," the grandmother said.

"Yes, Grandmother," said Eréndira.

The back room was a kind of shed with four brick columns, a roof of rotted palm leaves, and an adobe wall three feet high, through which outdoor disturbances got into the building. Placed on top of the adobe wall were pots with cacti and other plants of aridity. Hanging between two columns and flapping like the free sail of a drifting sloop was a faded hammock. Over the whistle of the storm and the lash of the water one could hear distant shouts, the howling of far-off animals, the cries of a shipwreck.

When Eréndira and the widower went into the shed they had to hold on so as not to be knocked down by a gust of rain which left them soaked. Their voices could not be heard but their movements became clear in the roar of the squall. At the widower's first attempt, Eréndira shouted something inaudible and tried to get away. The widower answered her without any voice, twisted her arm by the wrist, and dragged her to the hammock. She fought him off with a scratch on the face and shouted in silence again, but he replied with a solemn slap which lifted her off the ground and suspended her in the air for an instant with her long Medusa hair floating in space. He grabbed her about the waist before she touched ground again, flung her into the hammock with a brutal heave, and held her down with his knees. Eréndira then succumbed to terror, lost consciousness, and remained as if fascinated by the moonbeams from a fish that was floating through the storm air, while the widower undressed her, tearing off her clothes with a methodical clawing, as if he were pulling up grass, scattering them with great tugs of color that waved like streamers and went off with the wind.

When there was no other man left in the village who could pay anything for Eréndira's love, her grandmother put her on a truck to go where the smugglers were. They made the trip on the back of the truck in the open, among sacks of rice and buckets of lard and what had been left by the fire: the headboard of the viceregal bed, a warrior angel, the scorched throne, and other pieces of useless junk. In a trunk with two crosses painted in broad strokes they carried the bones of the Amadíses.

The grandmother protected herself from the sun with a tattered umbrella and it was hard for her to breathe because of the torment of sweat and dust, but even in that unhappy state she kept control of her dignity. Behind the pile of cans and sacks of rice Eréndira paid for the trip and the cartage by making love for twenty pesos a turn with the truck's loader. At first her system of defense was the same as she had used against the widower's attack, but the loader's approach was different, slow and wise, and he ended up taming her with tenderness. So when they reached the first town after a deadly journey, Eréndira and the loader were relaxing from good love behind the parapet of cargo. The driver shouted to the grandmother:

"Here's where the world begins."

The grandmother observed with disbelief the miserable and solitary streets of a town somewhat larger but just as sad as the one they had abandoned.

"It doesn't look like it to me," she said.

"It's mission country," the driver said.

"I'm not interested in charity, I'm interested in smugglers," said the grandmother.

Listening to the dialogue from behind the load, Eréndira dug into a sack of rice with her finger. Suddenly she found a string, pulled on it, and drew out a necklace of genuine pearls. She looked at it amazed, holding it between her fingers like a dead snake, while the driver answered her grandmother:

"Don't be daydreaming, ma'am. There's no such thing as smugglers."

"Of course not," the grandmother said. "I've got your word for it."

"Try to find one and you'll see," the driver bantered.

"Everybody talks about them, but no one's ever seen one."

The loader realized that Eréndira had pulled out the necklace and hastened to take it away from her and stick it back into the sack of rice. The grandmother, who had decided to stay in spite of the poverty of the town, then called to her granddaughter to help her out of the truck. Eréndira said good-bye to the loader with a kiss that was hurried but spontaneous and true.

The grandmother waited, sitting on her throne in the middle of the street, until they finished unloading the goods. The last item was the trunk with the remains of the Amadíses.

"This thing weighs as much as a dead man," said the driver, laughing.

"There are two of them," the grandmother said, "so treat them with the proper respect."

"I bet they're marble statutes." The driver laughed again.

He put the trunk with bones down carelessly among the singed furniture and held out his open hand to the grandmother.

"Fifty pesos," he said.

"Your slave has already paid on the right-hand side."

The driver looked at his helper with surprise and the latter made an affirmative sign. The driver then went back to the cab, where a woman in mourning was riding, in her arms a baby who was crying from the heat. The loader, quite sure of himself, told the grandmother:

"Eréndira is coming with me, if it's all right by you. My intentions are honorable."

The girl intervened, surprised:

"I didn't say anything!"

"The idea was all mine," the loader said.

The grandmother looked him up and down, not to make him feel small but trying to measure the true size of his guts.

"It's all right by me," she told him, "provided you pay me what I lost because of her carelessness. It's eight hundred seventy-two thousand three hundred fifteen pesos, less the four hundred and twenty which she's already paid me, making it eight hundred seventy-one thousand eight hundred ninety-five."

The truck started up.

"Believe me, I'd give you that pile of money if I had it," the loader said seriously. "The girl is worth it."

The grandmother was pleased with the boy's decision.

"Well, then, come back when you have it, son," she answered in a sympathetic tone. "But you'd better go now, because if we figure out accounts again you'll end up owing me ten pesos."

The loader jumped onto the back of the truck and it went off. From there he waved good-bye to Eréndira, but she was still so surprised that she didn't answer him.

In the same vacant lot where the truck had left them, Eréndira and her grandmother improvised a shelter to live in from sheets of zinc and the remains of Oriental rugs. They laid two mats on the ground and slept as well as they had in the mansion until the sun opened holes in the ceiling and burned their faces.

Just the opposite of what normally happened, it was the grandmother who busied herself that morning fixing up Eréndira. She made up her face in the style of sepulchral beauty that had been the vogue in her youth and touched her up with artificial fingernails and an organdy bow that looked like a butterfly on her head.

"You look awful," she admitted, "but it's better that way: men are quite stupid when it comes to female matters."

Long before they saw them they both recognized the sound of two mules walking on the flint of the desert. At a command from her grandmother, Eréndira lay down on the mat the way an amateur actress might have done at the moment when the curtain was about to go up. Leaning on her bishop's crosier, the grandmother went out of the shelter and sat down on the throne to wait for the mules to pass.

The mailman was coming. He was only twenty years old, but his work had aged him, and he was wearing a khaki uniform, leggings, a pith helmet, and had a military pistol on his cartridge belt. He was riding a good mule and leading by the halter another, more timeworn one, on whom the canvas mailbags were piled.

As he passed by the grandmother he saluted her and kept on going, but she signaled him to look inside the shelter. The man stopped and saw Eréndira lying on the mat in her posthumous make-up and wearing a purple-trimmed dress.

"Do you like it?" the grandmother asked.

The mailman hadn't understood until then what the proposition was.

"It doesn't look bad to someone who's been on a diet," he said, smiling.

"Fifty pesos," the grandmother said.

"Boy, you're asking a mint!" he said. "I can eat for a whole month on that."

"Don't be a tightwad," the grandmother said. "The airmail pays even better than being a priest."

"I'm the domestic mail," the man said. "The airmail man travels in a pickup truck."

"In any case, love is just as important as eating," the grandmother said.

"But it doesn't feed you."

The grandmother realized that a man who lived from what other people were waiting for had more than enough time for bargaining.

"How much have you got?" she asked him.

The mailman dismounted, took some chewed-up bills from his pocket, and showed them to the grandmother. She snatched them up all together with a rapid hand just as if they had been a ball.

"I'll lower the price for you," she said, "but on one condition: that you spread the word all around."

"All the way to the other side of the world," the mailman said. "That's what I'm for."

Eréndira, who had been unable to blink, then took off her artificial eyelashes and moved to one side of the mat to make room for the chance boyfriend. As soon as he was in the shelter, the grandmother closed the entrance with an energetic tug on the sliding curtain.

It was an effective deal. Taken by the words of the mailman, men came from very far away to become acquainted with the newness of Eréndira. Behind the men came gambling tables and food stands, and behind them all came a photographer on a bicycle, who, across from the encampment, set up a camera with a mourning sleeve on a tripod and a backdrop of a lake with listless swans.

The grandmother, fanning herself on her throne, seemed alien to her own bazaar. The only thing that interested her was keeping order in the line of customers who were waiting their turn and checking the exact amount of money they paid in advance to go in to Eréndira. At first she had been so strict that she refused a good customer because he was five pesos short. But with the passage of months she was assimilating the lessons of reality and she ended up letting people in who completed their payment with religious medals, family relics, wedding rings, and anything her bite could prove was bona-fide gold even if it didn't shine.

After a long stay in that first town, the grandmother had sufficient money to buy a donkey, and she went off into the desert in search of places more propitious for the payment of the debt. She traveled on a litter that had been improvised on top of the donkey and she was protected from the motionless sun by the half-spoked umbrella that Eréndira held over her head. Behind them walked four Indian bearers with the remnants of the encampment: the sleeping mats, the restored throne, the alabaster angel, and the trunks with the remains of the Amadíses. The photographer followed the caravan on his bicycle, but never catching up, as if he were going to a different festival.

Six months had passed since the fire when the grandmother was able to get a complete picture of the business.

"If things go on like this," she told Eréndira, "you will have paid me the debt inside of eight years, seven months, and eleven days."

She went back over her calculations with her eyes closed, fumbling with the seeds she was taking out of a cord pouch where she also kept the money, and she corrected herself:

"All that, of course, not counting the pay and board of the Indians and other minor expenses."

Eréndira, who was keeping in step with the donkey,

bowed down by the heat and dust, did not reproach her grandmother for her figures, but she had to hold back her tears.

"I've got ground glass in my bones," she said.

"Try to sleep."

"Yes, Grandmother."

She closed her eyes, took in a deep breath of scorching air, and went on walking in her sleep.

A small truck loaded with cages appeared, frightening goats in the dust of the horizon, and the clamor of the birds was like a splash of cool water for the Sunday torpor of San Miguel del Desierto. At the wheel was a corpulent Dutch farmer, his skin splintered by the outdoors, and with a squirrel-colored mustache he had inherited from some great-grandfather. His son Ulises, who was riding in the other seat, was a gilded adolescent with lonely maritime eyes and with the appearance of a furtive angel. The Dutchman noticed a tent in front of which all the soldiers of the local garrison were awaiting their turn. They were sitting on the ground, drinking out of the same bottle, which passed from mouth to mouth, and they had almond branches on their heads as if camouflaged for combat. The Dutchman asked in his language:

"What the devil can they be selling there?"

"A woman," his son answered quite naturally. "Her name is Eréndira."

"How do you know?"

"Everybody in the desert knows," Ulises answered.

The Dutchman stopped at the small hotel in town and got out. Ulises stayed in the truck. With agile fingers he

opened a briefcase that his father had left on the seat, took
out a roll of bills, put several in his pocket, and left everything just the way it had been. That night, while his father
was asleep, he climbed out the hotel window and went to
stand in line in front of Eréndira's tent.

The festivities were at their height. The drunken recruits
were dancing by themselves so as not to waste the free
music, and the photographer was taking nighttime pictures
with magnesium papers. As she watched over her business,
the grandmother counted the bank notes in her lap, divid-
ing them into equal piles and arranging them in a basket.
There were only twelve soldiers at that time, but the evening line had grown with civilian customers. Ulises was the
last one.

It was the turn of a soldier with a woeful appearance. The
grandmother not only blocked his way but avoided contact
with his money.

"No, son," she told him. "You couldn't go in for all the
gold in the world. You bring bad luck."

The soldier, who wasn't from those parts, was puzzled.

"What do you mean?"

"You bring down the evil shadows," the grandmother
said. "A person only has to look at your face."

She waved him off with her hand, but without touching
him, and made way for the next soldier.

"Go right in, handsome," she told him good-naturedly,
"but don't take too long, your country needs you."

The soldier went in but he came right out again because
Eréndira wanted to talk to her grandmother. She hung the
basket of money on her arm and went into the tent, which
wasn't very roomy, but which was neat and clean. In the

back, on an army cot, Eréndira was unable to repress the trembling in her body, and she was in sorry shape, all dirty with soldier sweat.

"Grandmother," she sobbed, "I'm dying."

The grandmother felt her forehead and when she saw she had no fever, she tried to console her.

"There are only ten soldiers left," she said.

Eréndira began to weep with the shrieks of a frightened animal. The grandmother realized then that she had gone beyond the limits of horror and, stroking her head, she helped her calm down.

"The trouble is that you're weak," she told her. "Come on, don't cry any more, take a bath in sage water to get your blood back into shape."

She left the tent when Eréndira was calmer and she gave the soldier waiting his money back. "That's all for today," she told him. "Come back tomorrow and I'll give you the first place in line." Then she shouted to those lined up:

"That's all, boys. Tomorrow morning at nine."

Soldiers and civilians broke ranks with shouts of protest. The grandmother confronted them, in a good mood but brandishing the devastating crosier in earnest.

"You're an inconsiderate bunch of slobs!" she shouted. "What do you think the girl is made of, iron? I'd like to see you in her place. You perverts! You shitty bums!"

The men answered her with even cruder insults, but she ended up controlling the revolt and stood guard with her staff until they took away the snack tables and dismantled the gambling stands. She was about to go back into the tent when she saw Ulises, as large as life, all by himself in the dark and empty space where the line of men had been before. He had an unreal aura about him and he seemed to be visible in the shadows because of the very glow of his beauty.

"You," the grandmother asked him. "What happened to your wings?"

"The one who had wings was my grandfather," Ulises answered in his natural way, "but nobody believed it."

The grandmother examined him again with fascination. "Well, I do," she said. "Put them on and come back tomorrow." She went into the tent and left Ulises burning where he stood.

Eréndira felt better after her bath. She had put on a short, lace-trimmed slip and she was drying her hair before going to bed, but she was still making an effort to hold back her tears. Her grandmother was asleep.

Behind Eréndira's bed, very slowly, Ulises' head appeared. She saw the anxious and diaphanous eyes, but before saying anything she rubbed her head with the towel in order to prove that it wasn't an illusion. When Ulises blinked for the first time, Eréndira asked him in a very low voice:

"Who are you?"

Ulises showed himself down to his shoulders. "My name is Ulises," he said. He showed her the bills he had stolen and added:

"I've got money."

Eréndira put her hands on the bed, brought her face close to that of Ulises, and went on talking to him as if in a kindergarten game.

"You were supposed to get in line," she told him.

"I waited all night long," Ulises said.

"Well, now you have to wait until tomorrow," Eréndira said. "I feel as if someone had been beating me on the kidneys."

At that instant the grandmother began to talk in her sleep.

"It's going on twenty years since it rained last," she said. "It was such a terrible storm that the rain was all mixed in with sea water, and the next morning the house was full of fish and snails and your grandfather Amadís, may he rest in peace, saw a glowing manta ray floating through the air."

Ulises hid behind the bed again. Eréndira showed an amused smile.

"Take it easy," she told him. "She always acts kind of crazy when she's asleep, but not even an earthquake can wake her up."

Ulises reappeared. Eréndira looked at him with a smile that was naughty and even a little affectionate and took the soiled sheet off the mattress.

"Come," she said. "Help me change the sheet."

Then Ulises came from behind the bed and took one end of the sheet. Since the sheet was much larger than the mattress, they had to fold it several times. With every fold Ulises drew closer to Eréndira.

"I was going crazy wanting to see you," he suddenly said. "Everybody says you're very pretty and they're right."

"But I'm going to die," Eréndira said.

"My mother says that people who die in the desert don't go to heaven but to the sea," Ulises said.

Eréndira put the dirty sheet aside and covered the mattress with another, which was clean and ironed.

"I never saw the sea," she said.

"It's like the desert but with water," said Ulises.

"Then you can't walk on it."

"My father knew a man who could," Ulises said, "but that was a long time ago."

Eréndira was fascinated but she wanted to sleep.

"If you come very early tomorrow you can be first in line," she said.

"I'm leaving with my father at dawn," said Ulises.

"Won't you be coming back this way?"

"Who can tell?" Ulises said. "We just happened along now because we got lost on the road to the border."

Eréndira looked thoughtfully at her sleeping grandmother.

"All right," she decided. "Give me the money."

Ulises gave it to her. Eréndira lay down on the bed but he remained trembling where he was: at the decisive moment his determination had weakened. Eréndira took him by the hand to hurry him up and only then did she notice his tribulation. She was familiar with that fear.

"Is it the first time?" she asked him.

Ulises didn't answer but he smiled in desolation. Eréndira became a different person.

"Breathe slowly," she told him. "That's the way it always is the first time. Afterwards you won't even notice."

She laid him down beside her and while she was taking his clothes off she was calming him maternally.

"What's your name?"

"Ulises."

"That's a gringo name," Eréndira said.

"No, a sailor name."

Eréndira uncovered his chest, gave a few little orphan kisses, sniffed him.

"It's like you were made of gold all over," she said, "but you smell of flowers."

"It must be the oranges," Ulises said.

Calmer now, he gave a smile of complicity.

"We carry a lot of birds along to throw people off the track," he added, "but what we're doing is smuggling a load of oranges across the border."

"Oranges aren't contraband," Eréndira said.

"These are," said Ulises. "Each one is worth fifty thousand pesos."

Eréndira laughed for the first time in a long while.

"What I like about you," she said, "is the serious way you make up nonsense."

She had become spontaneous and talkative again, as if Ulises' innocence had changed not only her mood but her character. The grandmother, such a short distance away from misfortune, was still talking in her sleep.

"Around those times, at the beginning of March, they brought you home," she said. "You looked like a lizard wrapped in cotton. Amadís, your father, who was young and handsome, was so happy that afternoon that he sent for twenty carts loaded with flowers and arrived strewing them along the street until the whole village was gold with flowers like the sea."

She ranted on with great shouts and with a stubborn passion for several hours. But Ulises couldn't hear her because Eréndira had loved him so much and so truthfully that she loved him again for half price while her grandmother was raving and kept on loving him for nothing until dawn.

A group of missionaries holding up their crucifixes stood shoulder to shoulder in the middle of the desert. A wind as fierce as the wind of misfortune shook their burlap habits and their rough beards and they were barely able to stand on their feet. Behind them was the mission, a colonial pile of stone with a tiny belfry on top of the harsh whitewashed walls.

The youngest missionary, who was in charge of the group, pointed to a natural crack in the glazed clay ground.

"You shall not pass beyond this line!" he shouted.

The four Indian bearers carrying the grandmother in a litter made of boards stopped when they heard the shout. Even though she was uncomfortable sitting on the planks of the litter and her spirit was dulled by the dust and sweat of the desert, the grandmother maintained her haughtiness intact. Eréndira was on foot. Behind the litter came a file of eight Indians carrying the baggage and at the very end the photographer on his bicycle.

"The desert doesn't belong to anyone," the grandmother said.

"It belongs to God," the missionary said, "and you are violating his sacred laws with your filthy business."

The grandmother then recognized the missionary's peninsular usage and diction and avoided a head-on confrontation so as not to break her head against his intransigence. She went back to being herself.

"I don't understand your mysteries, son."

The missionary pointed at Eréndira.

"That child is underage."

"But she's my granddaughter."

"So much the worse," the missionary replied. "Put her

under our care willingly or we'll have to seek recourse in
other ways."

The grandmother had not expected them to go so far.

"All right, if that's how it is." She surrendered in fear.
"But sooner or later I'll pass, you'll see."

Three days after the encounter with the missionaries, the
grandmother and Eréndira were sleeping in a village near
the mission when a group of stealthy, mute bodies, creep-
ing along like an infantry patrol, slipped into the tent. They
were six Indian novices, strong and young, their rough
cloth habits seeming to glow in the moonlight. Without
making a sound they cloaked Eréndira in a mosquito net-
ting, picked her up without waking her, and carried her off
wrapped like a large, fragile fish caught in a lunar net.

There were no means left untried by the grandmother in
an attempt to rescue her granddaughter from the protection of the missionaries. Only when they had all failed, from
the most direct to the most devious, did she turn to the civil
authority, which was vested in a military man. She found
him in the courtyard of his home, his chest bare, shooting
with an army rifle at a dark and solitary cloud in the burning
sky. He was trying to perforate it to bring on rain, and his
shots were furious and useless, but he did take the necessary time out to listen to the grandmother.

"I can't do anything," he explained to her when he had
heard her out. "The priesties, according to the concordat,
have the right to keep the girl until she comes of age. Or
until she gets married."

"Then why do they have you here as mayor?" the grandmother asked.

"To make it rain," was the mayor's answer.

Then, seeing that the cloud had moved out of range, he

interrupted his official duties and gave his full attention to the grandmother.

"What you need is someone with a lot of weight who will vouch for you," he told her. "Someone who can swear to your moral standing and your good behavior in a signed letter. Do you know Senator Onésimo Sánchez?"

Sitting under the naked sun on a stool that was too narrow for her astral buttocks, the grandmother answered with a solemn rage:

"I'm just a poor woman all alone in the vastness of the desert."

The mayor, his right eye twisted from the heat, looked at her with pity.

"Then don't waste your time, ma'am," he said. "You'll rot in hell."

She didn't rot, of course. She set up her tent across from the mission and sat down to think, like a solitary warrior besieging a fortified city. The wandering photographer, who knew her quite well, loaded his gear onto the carrier of his bicycle and was ready to leave all alone when he saw her in the full sun with her eyes fixed on the mission.

"Let's see who gets tired first," the grandmother said, "they or I."

"They've been here for three hundred years and they can still take it," the photographer said. "I'm leaving."

Only then did the grandmother notice the loaded bicycle.

"Where are you going?"

"Wherever the wind takes me," the photographer said, and he left. "It's a big world."

The grandmother sighed.

"Not as big as you think, you ingrate."

But she didn't move her head in spite of her anger so as not to lose sight of the mission. She didn't move it for many, many days of mineral heat, for many, many nights of wild winds, for all the time she was meditating and no one came out of the mission. The Indians built a lean-to of palm leaves beside the tent and hung their hammocks there, but the grandmother stood watch until very late, nodding on her throne and chewing the uncooked grain in her pouch with the invincible laziness of a resting ox.

One night a convoy of slow covered trucks passed very close to her and the only lights they carried were wreaths of colored bulbs which gave them the ghostly size of sleep-walking altars. The grandmother recognized them at once because they were just like the trucks of the Amadíses. The last truck in the convoy slowed, stopped, and a man got out of the cab to adjust something in back. He looked like a replica of the Amadíses, wearing a hat with a turned-up brim, high boots, two crossed cartridge belts across his chest, an army rifle, and two pistols. Overcome by an irresistible temptation, the grandmother called to the man.

"Don't you know who I am?" she asked him.

The man lighted her pitilessly with a flashlight. For an instant he studied the face worn out by vigil, the eyes dim from fatigue, the withered hair of the woman who, even at her age, in her sorry state, and with that crude light on her face, could have said that she had been the most beautiful woman in the world. When he examined her enough to be sure that he had never seen her before, he turned out the light.

"The only thing I know for sure is that you're not the Virgin of Perpetual Help."

"Quite the contrary," the grandmother said with a very

sweet voice. "I'm the Lady."

The man put his hand to his pistol out of pure instinct. "What lady?"

"Big Amadís's."

"Then you're not of this world," he said, tense. "What is it you want?"

"For you to help me rescue my granddaughter, Big Amadís's granddaughter, the daughter of our son Amadís, held captive in that mission."

The man overcame his fear.

"You knocked on the wrong door," he said. "If you think we're about to get mixed up in God's affairs, you're not the one you say you are, you never knew the Amadíses, and you haven't got the whoriest notion of what smuggling's all about."

Early that morning the grandmother slept less than before. She lay awake pondering things, wrapped in a wool blanket while the early hour got her memory all mixed up and the repressed raving struggled to get out even though she was awake, and she had to tighten her heart with her hand so as not to be suffocated by the memory of a house by the sea with great red flowers where she had been happy. She remained that way until the mission bell rang and the first lights went on in the windows and the desert became saturated with the smell of the hot bread of matins. Only then did she abandon her fatigue, tricked by the illusion that Eréndira had got up and was looking for a way to escape and come back to her.

Eréndira, however, had not lost a single night's sleep since they had taken her to the mission. They had cut her hair with pruning shears until her head was like a brush, they put a hermit's rough cassock on her and gave her a

bucket of whitewash and a broom so that she could whitewash the stairs every time someone went up or down. It was
mule work because there was an incessant coming and
going of muddied missionaries and novice carriers, but
Eréndira felt as if every day were Sunday after the fearsome
galley that had been her bed. Besides, she wasn't the only
one worn out at night, because that mission was dedicated
to fighting not against the devil but against the desert.
Eréndira had seen the Indian novices bulldogging cows in
the barn in order to milk them, jumping up and down on
planks for days on end in order to press cheese, helping a
goat through a difficult birth. She had seen them sweat like
tanned stevedores hauling water from the cistern, watering
by hand a bold garden that other novices cultivated with
hoes in order to plant vegetables in the flintstone of the
desert. She had seen the earthly inferno of the ovens for
baking bread and the rooms for ironing clothes. She had
seen a nun chase a pig through the courtyard, slide along
holding the runaway animal by the ears, and roll in a mud
puddle without letting go until two novices in leather
aprons helped her get it under control and one of them cut
its throat with a butcher knife as they all became covered
with blood and mire. In the isolation ward of the infirmary
she had seen tubercular nuns in their nightgown shrouds,
waiting for God's last command as they embroidered bridal
sheets on the terraces while the men preached in the desert. Eréndira was living in her shadows and discovering
other forms of beauty and horror that she had never imagined in the narrow world of her bed, but neither the coars-
est nor the most persuasive of the novices had managed to
get her to say a word since they had taken her to the mission. One morning, while she was preparing the whitewash

in her bucket, she heard string music that was like a light even more diaphanous than the light of the desert. Captivated by the miracle, she peeped into an immense and empty salon with bare walls and large windows through which the dazzling June light poured in and remained still, and in the center of the room she saw a very beautiful nun whom she had never seen before playing an Easter oratorio on the clavichord. Eréndira listened to the music without blinking, her heart hanging by a thread, until the lunch bell rang. After eating, while she whitewashed the stairs with her reed brush, she waited until all the novices had finished going up and coming down, and she was alone, with no one to hear her, and then she spoke for the first time since she had entered the mission.

"I'm happy," she said.

So that put an end to the hopes the grandmother had that Eréndira would run away to rejoin her, but she maintained her granite siege without having made any decision until Pentecost. During that time the missionaries were combing the desert in search of pregnant concubines in order to get them married. They traveled all the way to the most remote settlements in a broken-down truck with four well-armed soldiers and a chest of cheap cloth. The most difficult part of that Indian hunt was to convince the women, who defended themselves against divine grace with the truthful argument that men, sleeping in their hammocks with legs spread, felt they had the right to demand much heavier work from legitimate wives than from concubines. It was necessary to seduce them with trickery, dissolving the will of God in the syrup of their own language so that it would seem less harsh to them, but even the most crafty of them ended up being convinced by a pair of flashy earrings. The men, on the other hand, once the women's acceptance had been obtained, were routed out of their hammocks with rifle butts, bound, and hauled away in the back of the truck to be married by force.

For several days the grandmother saw the little truck loaded with pregnant Indian women heading for the mission, but she failed to recognize her opportunity. She recognized it on Pentecost Sunday itself, when she heard the rockets and the ringing of the bells and saw the miserable and merry crowd that was going to the festival, and she saw that among the crowds there were pregnant women with the veil and crown of a bride holding the arms of their casual mates, whom they would legitimize in the collective wedding.

Among the last in the procession a boy passed, innocent of heart, with gourd-cut Indian hair and dressed in rags, carrying an Easter candle with a silk bow in his hand. The grandmother called him over.

"Tell me something, son," she asked with her smoothest voice. "What part do you have in this affair?"

The boy felt intimidated by the candle and it was hard for him to close his mouth because of his donkey teeth.

"The priests are going to give me my first communion," he said.

"How much did they pay you?"

"Five pesos."

The grandmother took a roll of bills from her pouch and the boy looked at them with surprise.

"I'm going to give you twenty," the grandmother said. "Not for you to make your first communion, but for you to get married."

"Who to?"

"My granddaughter."

So Eréndira was married in the courtyard of the mission
in her hermit's cassock and a silk shawl that the novices
gave her, and without even knowing the name of the groom
her grandmother had bought for her. With uncertain hope
she withstood the torment of kneeling on the saltpeter
ground, the goat-hair stink of the two hundred pregnant
brides, the punishment of the Epistle of Saint Paul ham-
mered out in Latin under the motionless and burning sun,
because the missionaries had found no way to oppose the
wile of that unforeseen marriage, but had given her a promise as a last attempt to keep her in the mission. Nevertheless, after the ceremony in the presence of the apostolic
prefect, the military mayor who shot at the clouds, her
recent husband, and her impassive grandmother, Eréndira
found herself once more under the spell that had domi-
nated her since birth. When they asked her what her free,
true, and definitive will was, she didn't even give a sigh of
hesitation.

"I want to leave," she said. And she clarified things by
pointing at her husband. "But not with him, with my grandmother."

Ulises had wasted a whole afternoon trying to steal an
orange from his father's grove, because the older man
wouldn't take his eyes off him while they were pruning the
sick trees, and his mother kept watch from the house. So
he gave up his plan, for that day at least, and grudgingly
helped his father until they had pruned the last orange
trees.

The extensive grove was quiet and hidden, and the
wooden house with a tin roof had copper grating over the

windows and a large porch set on pilings, with primitive plants bearing intense flowers. Ulises' mother was on the porch sitting back in a Viennese rocking chair with smoked leaves on her temples to relieve her headache, and her full-blooded-Indian look followed her son like a beam of invisible light to the most remote corners of the orange grove. She was quite beautiful, much younger than her husband, and not only did she still wear the garb of her tribe, but she knew the most ancient secrets of her blood.

When Ulises returned to the house with the pruning tools, his mother asked him for her four o'clock medicine, which was on a nearby table. As soon as he touched them, the glass and the bottle changed color. Then, out of pure play, he touched a glass pitcher that was on the table beside some tumblers and the pitcher also turned blue. His mother observed him while she was taking her medicine and when she was sure that it was not a delirium of her pain, she asked him in the Guajiro Indian language:

"How long has that been happening to you?"

"Ever since we came back from the desert," Ulises said, also in Guajiro. "It only happens with glass things."

In order to demonstrate, one after the other he touched the glasses that were on the table and they all turned different colors.

"Those things happen only because of love," his mother said. "Who is it?"

Ulises didn't answer. His father, who couldn't understand the Guajiro language, was passing by the porch at that moment with a cluster of oranges.

"What are you two talking about?" he asked Ulises in Dutch.

"Nothing special," Ulises answered.

Ulises' mother didn't know any Dutch. When her husband went into the house, she asked her son in Guajiro:

"What did he say?"

"Nothing special," Ulises answered.

He lost sight of his father when he went into the house, but he saw him again through a window of the office. The mother waited until she was alone with Ulises and then repeated:

"Tell me who it is."

"It's nobody," Ulises said.

He answered without paying attention because he was hanging on his father's movements in the office. He had seen him put the oranges on top of the safe when he worked out the combination. But while he was keeping an eye on his father, his mother was keeping an eye on him.

"You haven't eaten any bread for a long time," she observed.

"I don't like it."

The mother's face suddenly took on an unaccustomed liveliness. "That's a lie," she said. "It's because you're lovesick and people who are lovesick can't eat bread." Her voice, like her eyes, had passed from entreaty to threat.

"It would be better if you told me who it was," she said, "or I'll make you take some purifying baths."

In the office the Dutchman opened the safe, put the oranges inside, and closed the armored door. Ulises moved away from the window then and answered his mother impatiently.

"I already told you there wasn't anyone," he said. "If you don't believe me, ask Papa."

The Dutchman appeared in the office doorway lighting his sailor's pipe and carrying his threadbare Bible under his arm. His wife asked him in Spanish:

"Who did you meet in the desert?"

"Nobody," her husband answered, a little in the clouds. "If you don't believe me, ask Ulises."

He sat down at the end of the hall and sucked on his pipe until the tobacco was used up. Then he opened the Bible at random and recited spot passages for almost two hours in flowing and ringing Dutch.

At midnight Ulises was still thinking with such intensity that he couldn't sleep. He rolled about in his hammock for another hour, trying to overcome the pain of memories until the very pain gave him the strength he needed to make a decision. Then he put on his cowboy pants, his plaid shirt, and his riding boots, jumped through the window, and fled from the house in the truck loaded with birds. As he went through the groves he picked the three ripe oranges he had been unable to steal that afternoon.

He traveled across the desert for the rest of the night and at dawn he asked in towns and villages about the whereabouts of Eréndira, but no one could tell him. Finally they informed him that she was traveling in the electoral campaign retinue of Senator Onésimo Sánchez and that on that day he was probably in Nueva Castilla. He didn't find him there but in the next town and Eréndira was no longer with him, for the grandmother had managed to get the senator to vouch for her morality in a letter written in his own hand, and with it she was going about opening the most tightly barred doors in the desert. On the third day he came across the domestic mailman and the latter told him what direction to follow.

"They're heading toward the sea," he said, "and you'd better hurry because the goddamned old woman plans to cross over to the island of Aruba."

Following that direction, after half a day's journey Ulises spotted the broad, stained tent that the grandmother had bought from a bankrupt circus. The wandering photographer had come back to her, convinced that the world was really not as large as he had thought, and he had set up his idyllic backdrops near the tent. A band of brass-blowers was captivating Eréndira's clientele with a taciturn waltz.

Ulises waited for his turn to go in, and the first thing that caught his attention was the order and cleanliness of the inside of the tent. The grandmother's bed had recovered its viceregal splendor, the statue of the angel was in its place beside the funerary trunk of the Amadíses, and in addition, there was a pewter bathtub with lion's feet. Lying on her new canopied bed, Eréndira was naked and placid, irradiating a childlike glow under the light that filtered through the tent. She was sleeping with her eyes open. Ulises stopped beside her, the oranges in his hand, and he noticed that she was looking at him without seeing him. Then he passed his hand over her eyes and called her by the name he had invented when he wanted to think about her:

"Arídnere."

Eréndira woke up. She felt naked in front of Ulises, let out a squeak, and covered herself with the sheet up to her neck.

"Don't look at me," she said. "I'm horrible."

"You're the color of an orange all over," Ulises said. He raised the fruits to her eyes so that she could compare. "Look."

Eréndira uncovered her eyes and saw that indeed the oranges did have her color.

"I don't want you to stay now," she said.

"I only came to show you this," Ulises said. "Look here."

He broke open an orange with his nails, split it in two with his hands, and showed Eréndira what was inside: stuck in the heart of the fruit was a genuine diamond.

"These are the oranges we take across the border," he said.

"But they're living oranges!" Eréndira exclaimed.

"Of course." Ulises smiled. "My father grows them."

Eréndira couldn't believe it. She uncovered her face, took the diamond in her fingers and contemplated it with surprise.

"With three like these we can take a trip around the world," Ulises said.

Eréndira gave him back the diamond with a look of disappointment. Ulises went on:

"Besides, I've got a pickup truck," he said. "And besides that . . . Look!"

From underneath his shirt he took an ancient pistol.

"I can't leave for ten years," Eréndira said.

"You'll leave," Ulises said. "Tonight, when the white whale falls asleep, I'll be outside there calling like an owl."

He made such a true imitation of the call of an owl that Eréndira's eyes smiled for the first time.

"It's my grandmother," she said.

"The owl?"

"The whale."

They both laughed at the mistake, but Eréndira picked up the thread again.

"No one can leave for anywhere without her grandmother's permission."

"There's no reason to say anything."

"She'll find out in any case," Eréndira said. "She can dream things."

"When she starts to dream that you're leaving we'll already be across the border. We'll cross over like smugglers," Ulises said.

Grasping the pistol with the confidence of a movie gunfighter, he imitated the sounds of the shots to excite Eréndira with his audacity. She didn't say yes or no, but her eyes gave a sigh and she sent Ulises away with a kiss. Ulises, touched, whispered:

"Tomorrow we'll be watching the ships go by."

That night, a little after seven o'clock, Eréndira was combing her grandmother's hair when the wind of her misfortune blew again. In the shelter of the tent were the Indian bearers and the leader of the brass band, waiting to be paid. The grandmother finished counting out the bills on a chest she had within reach, and after consulting a ledger she paid the oldest of the Indians.

"Here you are," she told him. "Twenty pesos for the week, less eight for meals, less three for water, less fifty cents on account for the new shirts, that's eight fifty. Count it."

The oldest Indian counted the money and they all withdrew with a bow.

"Thank you, white lady."

Next came the leader of the band. The grandmother consulted her ledger and turned to the photographer, who was trying to repair the bellows of his camera with wads of gutta-percha.

"What's it going to be?" she asked him. "Will you or won't you pay a quarter of the cost of the music?"

The photographer didn't even raise his head to answer.

"Music doesn't come out in pictures."

"But it makes people want to have their pictures taken," the grandmother answered.

"On the contrary," said the photographer. "It reminds them of the dead and then they come out in the picture with their eyes closed."

The bandleader intervened.

"What makes them close their eyes isn't the music," he said. "It's the lightning you make taking pictures at night."

"It's the music," the photographer insisted.

The grandmother put an end to the dispute. "Don't be a cheapskate," she said to the photographer. "Look how well things have been going for Senator Onésimo Sánchez and it's thanks to the musicians he has along." Then, in a harsh tone, she concluded:

"So pay what you ought to or go follow your fortune by yourself. It's not right for that poor child to carry the whole burden of expenses."

"I'll follow my fortune by myself," the photographer said. "After all, an artist is what I am."

The grandmother shrugged her shoulders and took care of the musician. She handed him a bundle of bills that matched the figure written in her ledger.

"Two hundred and fifty-four numbers," she told him. "At fifty cents apiece, plus thirty-two on Sundays and holidays at sixty cents apiece, that's one hundred fifty-six twenty."

The musician wouldn't accept the money.

"It's one hundred eighty-two forty," he said. "Waltzes cost more."

"Why is that?"

"Because they're sadder," the musician said.

The grandmother made him take the money.

"Well, this week you'll play us two happy numbers for each waltz I owe you for and we'll be even."

The musician didn't understand the grandmother's logic, but he accepted the figures while he unraveled the tangle. At that moment the fearsome wind threatened to uproot the tent, and in the silence that it left in its wake, outside, clear and gloomy, the call of an owl was heard.

Eréndira didn't know what to do to disguise her upset. She closed the chest with the money and hid it under the bed, but the grandmother recognized the fear in her hand when she gave her the key. "Don't be frightened," she told her. "There are always owls on windy nights." Still she didn't seem so convinced when she saw the photographer go out with the camera on his back.

"Wait till tomorrow if you'd like," she told him. "Death is on the loose tonight."

The photographer had also noticed the call of the owl, but he didn't change his intentions.

"Stay, son," the grandmother insisted. "Even if it's just because of the liking I have for you."

"But I won't pay for the music," the photographer said.

"Oh, no," the grandmother said. "Not that."

"You see?" the photographer said. "You've got no love for anybody."

The grandmother grew pale with rage.

"Then beat it!" she said. "You lowlife!"

She felt so outraged that she was still venting her rage on him while Eréndira helped her go to bed. "Son of an evil mother," she muttered. "What does that bastard know about anyone else's heart?" Eréndira paid no attention to her, because the owl was calling her with tenacious insistence during the pauses in the wind and she was tormented by uncertainty. The grandmother finally went to bed with the same ritual that had been *de rigueur* in the ancient mansion, and while her granddaughter fanned her she overcame her anger and once more breathed her sterile breath.

"You have to get up early," she said then, "so you can boil the infusion for my bath before the people get here."

"Yes, Grandmother."

"With the time you have left, wash the Indians' dirty laundry and that way we'll have something else to take off their pay next week."

"Yes, Grandmother," Eréndira said.

"And sleep slowly so that you won't get tired, because tomorrow is Thursday, the longest day of the week."

"Yes, Grandmother."

"And feed the ostrich."

"Yes, Grandmother," Eréndira said.

She left the fan at the head of the bed and lighted two altar candles in front of the chest with their dead. The grandmother, asleep now, was lagging behind with her orders.

"Don't forget to light the candles for the Amadíses."

"Yes, Grandmother."

Eréndira knew then that she wouldn't wake up, because she had begun to rave. She heard the wind barking about the tent, but she didn't recognize it as the wind of her misfortune that time either. She looked out into the night until the owl called again and her instinct for freedom in the end prevailed over her grandmother's spell.

She hadn't taken five steps outside the tent when she came across the photographer, who was lashing his equipment to the carrier of his bicycle. His accomplice's smile calmed her down.

"I don't know anything," the photographer said, "I haven't seen anything, and I won't pay for the music."

He took his leave with a blessing for all. Then Eréndira ran toward the desert, having decided once and for all, and she was swallowed up in the shadows of the wind where the owl was calling.

That time the grandmother went to the civil authorities at once. The commandant of the local detachment leaped out of his hammock at six in the morning when she put the senator's letter before his eyes. Ulises' father was waiting at the door.

"How in hell do you expect me to know what it says!" the commandant shouted. "I can't read."

"It's a letter of recommendation from Senator Onésimo Sánchez," the grandmother said.

Without further questions, the commandant took down a rifle he had near his hammock and began to shout orders to his men. Five minutes later they were all in a military truck flying toward the border against a contrary wind that had erased all trace of the fugitives. The commandant rode in the front seat beside the driver. In back were the Dutchman and the grandmother, with an armed policeman on each running board.

Close to town they stopped a convoy of trucks covered with waterproof canvases. Several men who were riding concealed in the rear raised the canvas and aimed at the small vehicle with machine guns and army rifles. The commandant asked the driver of the first truck how far back they had passed a farm truck loaded with birds.

The driver started up before he answered.

"We're not stool pigeons," he said indignantly, "we're smugglers."

The commandant saw the sooty barrels of the machine guns pass close to his eyes and he raised his arms and smiled.

"At least," he shouted at them, "you could have the decency not to go around in broad daylight."

The last truck had a sign on its rear bumper: I THINK OF YOU, ERÉNDIRA.

The wind became drier as they headed north and the sun was fiercer than the wind. It was hard to breathe because of the heat and dust inside the closed-in truck.

The grandmother was the first to spot the photographer: he was pedaling along in the same direction in which they were flying, with no protection against the sun except for a handkerchief tied around his head.

"There he is." She pointed. "He was their accomplice, the lowlife."

The commandant ordered one of the policemen on the running board to take charge of the photographer.

"Grab him and wait for us here," he said. "We'll be right back."

The policeman jumped off the running board and shouted twice for the photographer to halt. The photographer didn't hear him because of the wind blowing in the opposite direction. When the truck went on, the grandmother made an enigmatic gesture to him, but he confused it with a greeting, smiled, and waved. He didn't hear the shot. He flipped into the air and fell dead on top of his bicycle, his head blown apart by a rifle bullet, and he never knew where it came from.

Before noon they began to see feathers. They were passing by in the wind and they were feathers from young birds.
The Dutchman recognized them because they were from
his birds, plucked out by the wind. The driver changed
direction, pushed the gas pedal to the floor, and in half an
hour they could make out the pickup truck on the horizon.

When Ulises saw the military vehicle appear in the rear-
view mirror, he made an effort to increase the distance
between them, but the motor couldn't do any better. They
had traveled with no sleep and were done in from fatigue
and thirst. Eréndira, who was dozing on Ulises' shoulder,
woke up in fright. She saw the truck that was about to
overtake them and with innocent determination she took
the pistol from the glove compartment.

"It's no good," Ulises said. "It used to belong to Sir
Francis Drake."

She pounded it several times and threw it out the window. The military patrol passed the broken-down truck
loaded with birds plucked by the wind, turned sharply, and
cut it off.

It was around that time that I came to know them, their
moment of greatest splendor, but I wouldn't look into the
details of their lives until many years later when Rafael
Escalona, in a song, revealed the terrible ending of the
drama and I thought it would be good to tell the tale. I was
traveling about selling encyclopedias and medical books in
the province of Riohacha. Álvaro Cepeda Samudio, who
was also traveling in the region, selling beer-cooling equipment, took me through the desert towns in his truck with
the intention of talking to me about something and we
talked so much about nothing and drank so much beer that

without knowing when or where we crossed the entire desert and reached the border. There was the tent of wandering love under hanging canvas signs: ERÉNDIRA IS BEST;
LEAVE AND COME BACK—ERÉNDIRA WAITS FOR YOU; THERE'S
NO LIFE WITHOUT ERÉNDIRA. The endless wavy line com-
posed of men of diverse races and ranks looked like a snake
with human vertebrae dozing through vacant lots and
squares, through gaudy bazaars and noisy marketplaces,
coming out of the streets of that city, which was noisy with
passing merchants. Every street was a public gambling den,
every house a saloon, every doorway a refuge for fugitives.
The many undecipherable songs and the shouted offerings
of wares formed a single roar of panic in the hallucinating
heat.

Among the throng of men without a country and sharp-
ers was Blacamán the Good, up on a table and asking for
a real serpent in order to test an antidote of his invention
on his own flesh. There was the woman who had been
changed into a spider for having disobeyed her parents,
who would let herself be touched for fifty cents so that
people would see there was no trick, and she would answer
questions of those who might care to ask about her misfortune. There was an envoy from the eternal life who announced the imminent coming of the fearsome astral bat,
whose burning brimstone breath would overturn the order
of nature and bring the mysteries of the sea to the surface.

The one restful backwater was the red-light district,
reached only by the embers of the urban din. Women from
the four quadrants of the nautical rose yawned with bore-
dom in the abandoned cabarets. They had slept their sies-
tas sitting up, unawakened by people who wanted them,
and they were still waiting for the astral bat under the fans

that spun on the ceilings. Suddenly one of them got up and went to a balcony with pots of pansies that overlooked the street. Down there the row of Eréndira's suitors was passing.

"Come on," the woman shouted at them. "What's that one got that we don't have?"

"A letter from a senator," someone shouted.

Attracted by the shouts and the laughter, other women came out onto the balcony.

"The line's been like that for days," one of them said. "Just imagine, fifty pesos apiece."

The one who had come out first made a decision:

"Well, I'm going to go find out what jewel that seven-month baby has got."

"Me too," another said. "It'll be better than sitting here warming our chairs for free."

On the way others joined them and when they got to Eréndira's tent they made up a rowdy procession. They went in without any announcement, used pillows to chase away the man they found spending himself as best he could for his money, and they picked up Eréndira's bed and carried it out into the street like a litter.

"This is an outrage!" the grandmother shouted. "You pack of traitors, you bandits!" And then, turning to the men in line: "And you, you sissies, where do you keep your balls, letting this attack against a poor defenseless child go on? Damned fags!"

She kept on shouting as far as her voice would carry, distributing whacks with her crosier against all who came within reach, but her rage was inaudible amongst the shouts and mocking whistles of the crowd.

Eréndira couldn't escape the ridicule because she was

prevented by the dog chain that the grandmother used to hitch her to a slat of the bed ever since she had tried to run away. But they didn't harm her. They exhibited her on the canopied altar along the noisiest streets like the allegorical passage of the enchained penitent and finally they set her down like a catafalque in the center of the main square. Eréndira was all coiled up, her face hidden, but not weeping, and she stayed that way under the terrible sun in the square, biting with shame and rage at the dog chain of her evil destiny until someone was charitable enough to cover her with a shirt.

That was the only time I saw them, but I found out that they had stayed in that border town under the protection of the public forces until the grandmother's chests were bursting and then they left the desert and headed toward the sea. Never had such opulence been seen gathered together in that realm of poor people. It was a procession of ox-drawn carts on which cheap replicas of the paraphernalia lost in the disaster of the mansion were piled, not just the imperial busts and rare clocks, but also a secondhand piano and a Victrola with a crank and the records of nostalgia. A team of Indians took care of the cargo and a band of musicians announced their triumphal arrival in the villages.

The grandmother traveled on a litter with paper wreaths, chomping on the grains in her pouch, in the shadow of a church canopy. Her monumental size had increased, because under her blouse she was wearing a vest of sailcloth in which she kept the gold bars the way one keeps cartridges in a bandoleer. Eréndira was beside her, dressed in gaudy fabrics and with trinkets hanging, but with the dog chain still on her ankle.

"You've got no reason to complain," her grandmother had said to her when they left the border town. "You've got the clothes of a queen, a luxurious bed, a musical band of your own, and fourteen Indians at your service. Don't you think that's splendid?"

"Yes, Grandmother."

"When you no longer have me," the grandmother went on, "you won't be left to the mercy of men because you'll have your own home in an important city. You'll be free and happy."

It was a new and unforeseen vision of the future. On the other hand, she no longer spoke about the original debt, whose details had become twisted and whose installments had grown as the costs of the business became more complicated. Still Eréndira didn't let slip any sigh that would have given a person a glimpse of her thoughts. She submitted in silence to the torture of the bed in the saltpeter pits, in the torpor of the lakeside towns, in the lunar craters of the talcum mines, while her grandmother sang the vision of the future to her as if she were reading cards. One afternoon, as they came out of an oppressive canyon, they noticed a wind of ancient laurels and they caught snatches of Jamaica conversations and felt an urge to live and a knot in their hearts. They had reached the sea.

"There it is," the grandmother said, breathing in the glassy light of the Caribbean after half a lifetime of exile. "Don't you like it?"

"Yes, Grandmother."

They pitched the tent there. The grandmother spent the night talking without dreaming and sometimes she mixed up her nostalgia with clairvoyance of the future. She slept later than usual and awoke relaxed by the sound of the sea.

Nevertheless, when Eréndira was bathing her she again made predictions of the future and it was such a feverish clairvoyance that it seemed like the delirium of a vigil.

"You'll be a noble lady," she told her. "A lady of quality, venerated by those under your protection and favored and honored by the highest authorities. Ships' captains will send you postcards from every port in the world."

Eréndira wasn't listening to her. The warm water perfumed with oregano was pouring into the bathtub through a tube fed from outside. Eréndira picked it up in a gourd, impenetrable, not even breathing, and poured it over her grandmother with one hand while she soaped her with the other.

"The prestige of your house will fly from mouth to mouth from the string of the Antilles to the realm of Holland," the grandmother was saying. "And it will be more important than the presidential palace, because the affairs of government will be discussed there and the fate of the nation will be decided."

Suddenly the water in the tube stopped. Eréndira left the tent to find out what was going on and saw the Indian in charge of pouring water into the tube chopping wood by the kitchen.

"It ran out," the Indian said. "We have to cool more water."

Eréndira went to the stove, where there was another large pot with aromatic herbs boiling. She wrapped her hands in a cloth and saw that she could lift the pot without the help of the Indian.

"You can go," she told him. "I'll pour the water."

She waited until the Indian had left the kitchen. Then she took the boiling pot off the stove, lifted it with great effort to the height of the tube, and was about to pour the deadly water into the conduit to the bathtub when the grandmother shouted from inside the tent:

"Eréndira!"

It was as if she had seen. The granddaughter, frightened by the shout, repented at the last minute.

"Coming, Grandmother," she said. "I'm cooling off the water."

That night she lay thinking until quite late while her grandmother sang in her sleep, wearing the golden vest. Eréndira looked at her from her bed with intense eyes that in the shadows resembled those of a cat. Then she went to bed like a person who had drowned, her arms on her breast and her eyes open, and she called with all the strength of her inner voice:

"Ulises!"

Ulises woke up suddenly in the house on the orange plantation. He had heard Eréndira's voice so clearly that he was looking for her in the shadows of the room. After an instant of reflection, he made a bundle of his clothing and shoes and left the bedroom. He had crossed the porch when his father's voice surprised him:

"Where are you going?"

Ulises saw him blue in the moonlight.

"Into the world," he answered.

"This time I won't stop you," the Dutchman said. "But I warn you of one thing: wherever you go your father's curse will follow you."

"So be it," said Ulises.

Surprised and even a little proud of his son's resolution, the Dutchman followed him through the orange grove with a look that slowly began to smile. His wife was behind him

with her beautiful Indian woman's way of standing. The
Dutchman spoke when Ulises closed the gate.

"He'll be back," he said, "beaten down by life, sooner
than you think."

"You're so stupid," she sighed. "He'll never come back."

On that occasion Ulises didn't have to ask anyone where
Eréndira was. He crossed the desert hiding in passing
trucks, stealing to eat and sleep and stealing many times for
the pure pleasure of the risk until he found the tent in
another seaside town which the glass buildings gave the
look of an illuminated city and where resounded the noc-
turnal farewells of ships weighing anchor for the island of
Aruba. Eréndira was asleep chained to the slat and in the
same position of a drowned person on the beach from
which she had called him. Ulises stood looking at her for
a long time without waking her up, but he looked at her
with such intensity that Eréndira awoke. Then they kissed
in the darkness, caressed each other slowly, got undressed
wearily, with a silent tenderness and a hidden happiness
that was more than ever like love.

At the other end of the tent the sleeping grandmother
gave a monumental turn and began to rant.

"That was during the time the Greek ship arrived," she
said. "It was a crew of madmen who made the women
happy and didn't pay them with money but with sponges,
living sponges that later on walked about the houses moaning like patients in a hospital and making the children cry
so that they could drink the tears."

She made a subterranean movement and sat up in bed.

"That was when he arrived, my God," she shouted,
"stronger, taller, and much more of a man than Amadís."

Ulises, who until then had not paid any attention to the

raving, tried to hide when he saw the grandmother sitting up in bed. Eréndira calmed him.

"Take it easy," she told him. "Every time she gets to that part she sits up in bed, but she doesn't wake up."

Ulises leaned on her shoulder.

"I was singing with the sailors that night and I thought it was an earthquake," the grandmother went on. "They all must have thought the same thing because they ran away shouting, dying with laughter, and only he remained under the starsong canopy. I remember as if it had been yesterday that I was singing the song that everyone was singing those days. Even the parrots in the courtyard sang it."

Flat as a mat, as one can sing only in dreams, she sang the lines of her bitterness:

> *Lord, oh, Lord, give me back the innocence I had*
> *So I can feel his love all over again from the start.*

Only then did Ulises become interested in the grandmother's nostalgia.

"There he was," she was saying, "with a macaw on his shoulder and a cannibal-killing blunderbuss, the way Guatarral arrived in the Guianas, and I felt his breath of death when he stood opposite me and said: 'I've been around the world a thousand times and seen women of every nation, so I can tell you on good authority that you are the haughtiest and the most obliging, the most beautiful woman on earth.'"

She lay down again and sobbed on her pillow. Ulises and Eréndira remained silent for a long time, rocked in the shadows by the sleeping old woman's great breathing. Suddenly Eréndira, without the slightest quiver in her voice, asked:

"Would you dare to kill her?"

Taken by surprise, Ulises didn't know what to answer.

"Who knows," he said. "Would you dare?"

"I can't," Eréndira said. "She's my grandmother."

Then Ulises looked once more at the enormous sleeping body as if measuring its quantity of life and decided:

"For you I'd be capable of anything."

Ulises bought a pound of rat poison, mixed it with whipped cream and raspberry jam, and poured that fatal cream into a piece of pastry from which he had removed the original filling. Then he put some thicker cream on top, smoothing it with a spoon until there was no trace of his sinister maneuver, and he completed the trick with seventy-two little pink candles.

The grandmother sat up on her throne waving her threatening crosier when she saw him come into the tent with the birthday cake.

"You brazen devil!" she shouted. "How dare you set foot in this place?"

Ulises hid behind his angel face.

"I've come to ask your forgiveness," he said, "on this day, your birthday."

Disarmed by his lie, which had hit its mark, the grandmother had the table set as if for a wedding feast. She sat Ulises down on her right while Eréndira served them, and after blowing out the candles with one devastating gust, she cut the cake into two equal parts. She served Ulises.

"A man who knows how to get himself forgiven has earned half of heaven," she said. "I give you the first piece, which is the piece of happiness."

"I don't like sweet things," he said. "You take it."

The grandmother offered Eréndira a piece of cake. She took it into the kitchen and threw it in the garbage.

The grandmother ate the rest all by herself. She put whole pieces into her mouth and swallowed them without chewing, moaning with delight and looking at Ulises from the limbo of her pleasure. When there was no more on her plate she also ate what Ulises had turned down. While she was chewing the last bit, with her fingers she picked up the crumbs from the tablecloth and put them into her mouth.

She had eaten enough arsenic to exterminate a whole generation of rats. And yet she played the piano and sang until midnight, went to bed happy, and was able to have a normal sleep. The only thing new was a rocklike scratch in her breathing.

Eréndira and Ulises kept watch over her from the other bed, and they were only waiting for her death rattle. But the voice was as alive as ever when she began to rave.

"I went crazy, my God, I went crazy!" she shouted. "I put two bars on the bedroom door so he couldn't get in; I put the dresser and table against the door and the chairs on the table, and all he had to do was give a little knock with his ring for the defenses to fall apart, the chairs to fall off the table by themselves, the table and dresser to separate by themselves, the bars to move out of their slots by themselves."

Eréndira and Ulises looked at her with growing surprise as the delirium became more profound and dramatic and the voice more intimate.

"I felt I was going to die, soaked in the sweat of fear, begging inside for the door to open without opening, for him to enter without entering, for him never to go away but never to come back either so I wouldn't have to kill him!"

She went on repeating her drama for several hours, even the most intimate details, as if she had lived it again in her dream. A little before dawn she rolled over in bed with a movement of seismic accommodation and the voice broke with the imminence of sobs.

"I warned him and he laughed," she shouted. "I warned him again and he laughed again, until he opened his eyes in terror, saying, 'Agh, queen! Agh, queen!' and his voice wasn't coming out of his mouth but through the cut the knife had made in his throat."

Ulises, terrified at the grandmother's fearful evocation, grabbed Eréndira's hand.

"Murdering old woman!" he exclaimed.

Eréndira didn't pay any attention to him because at that instant dawn began to break. The clocks struck five.

"Go!" Eréndira said. "She's going to wake up now."

"She's got more life in her than an elephant," Ulises exclaimed. "It can't be!"

Eréndira cut him with a knifing look.

"The whole trouble," she said, "is that you're no good at all for killing anybody."

Ulises was so affected by the crudeness of the reproach that he left the tent. Eréndira kept on looking at the sleeping grandmother with her secret hate, with the rage of her frustration, as the sun rose and the bird air awakened. Then the grandmother opened her eyes and looked at her with a placid smile.

"God be with you, child."

The only noticeable change was a beginning of disorder in the daily routine. It was Wednesday, but the grandmother wanted to put on a Sunday dress, decided that Eréndira would receive no customers before eleven o'-

clock, and asked her to paint her nails garnet and give her a pontifical coiffure.

"I never had so much of an urge to have my picture taken," she exclaimed.

Eréndira began to comb her grandmother's hair, but as she drew the comb through the tangles a clump of hair remained between the teeth. She showed it to her grandmother in alarm. The grandmother examined it, pulled on another clump with her fingers, and another bush of hair was left in her hand. She threw it on the ground, tried again and pulled out a larger lock. Then she began to pull her hair with both hands, dying with laughter, throwing the handfuls into the air with an incomprehensible jubilation until her head looked like a peeled coconut.

Eréndira had no more news of Ulises until two weeks later when she caught the call of the owl outside the tent. The grandmother had begun to play the piano and was so absorbed in her nostalgia that she was unaware of reality. She had a wig of radiant feathers on her head.

Eréndira answered the call and only then did she notice the wick that came out of the piano and went on through the underbrush and was lost in the darkness. She ran to where Ulises was, hid next to him among the bushes, and with tight hearts they both watched the little blue flame that crept along the wick, crossed the dark space, and went into the tent.

"Cover your ears," Ulises said.

They both did, without any need, for there was no explosion. The tent lighted up inside with a radiant glow, burst in silence, and disappeared in a whirlwind of wet powder. When Eréndira dared enter, thinking that her grandmother was dead, she found her with her wig singed and her nightshirt in tatters, but more alive than ever, trying to put out the fire with a blanket.

Ulises slipped away under the protection of the shouts of the Indians, who didn't know what to do, confused by the grandmother's contradictory orders. When they finally managed to conquer the flames and get rid of the smoke, they were looking at a shipwreck.

"It's like the work of the evil one," the grandmother said. "Pianos don't explode just like that."

She made all kinds of conjectures to establish the causes of the new disaster, but Eréndira's evasions and her impassive attitude ended up confusing her. She couldn't find the slightest crack in her granddaughter's behavior, nor did she consider the existence of Ulises. She was awake until dawn, threading suppositions together and calculating the loss. She slept little and poorly. On the following morning, when Eréndira took the vest with the gold bars off her grandmother, she found fire blisters on her shoulders and raw flesh on her breast. "I had good reason to be turning over in my sleep," she said as Eréndira put egg whites on the burns. "And besides, I had a strange dream." She made an effort at concentration to evoke the image until it was as clear in her memory as in the dream.

"It was a peacock in a white hammock," she said.

Eréndira was surprised but she immediately assumed her everyday expression once more.

"It's a good sign," she lied. "Peacocks in dreams are animals with long lives."

"May God hear you," the grandmother said, "because we're back where we started. We have to begin all over again."

Eréndira didn't change her expression. She went out of

the tent with the plate of compresses and left her grandmother with her torso soaked in egg white and her skull
daubed with mustard. She was putting more egg whites
into the plate under the palm shelter that served as a
kitchen when she saw Ulises' eyes appear behind the stove
as she had seen them the first time behind her bed. She
wasn't startled, but told him in a weary voice:

"The only thing you've managed to do is increase my
debt."

Ulises' eyes clouded over with anxiety. He was motionless, looking at Eréndira in silence, watching her crack the
eggs with a fixed expression of absolute disdain, as if he
didn't exist. After a moment the eyes moved, looked over
the things in the kitchen, the hanging pots, the strings of
annatto, the carving knife. Ulises stood up, still not saying
anything, went in under the shelter, and took down the
knife.

Eréndira didn't look at him again, but when Ulises left
the shelter she told him in a very low voice:

"Be careful, because she's already had a warning of
death. She dreamed about a peacock in a white hammock."

The grandmother saw Ulises come in with the knife, and
making a supreme effort, she stood up without the aid of
her staff and raised her arms.

"Boy!" she shouted. "Have you gone mad?"

Ulises jumped on her and plunged the knife into her
naked breast. The grandmother moaned, fell on him, and
tried to strangle him with her powerful bear arms.

"Son of a bitch," she growled. "I discovered too late that
you have the face of a traitor angel."

She was unable to say anything more because Ulises
managed to free the knife and stab her a second time in the

side. The grandmother let out a hidden moan and hugged her attacker with more strength. Ulises gave her a third stab, without pity, and a spurt of blood, released by high pressure, sprinkled his face: it was oily blood, shiny and green, just like mint honey.

Eréndira appeared at the entrance with the plate in her hand and watched the struggle with criminal impassivity.

Huge, monolithic, roaring with pain and rage, the grandmother grasped Ulises' body. Her arms, her legs, even her hairless skull were green with blood. Her enormous bellows-breathing, upset by the first rattles of death, filled the whole area. Ulises managed to free his arm with the weapon once more, opened a cut in her belly, and an explosion of blood soaked him in green from head to toe. The grandmother tried to reach the open air which she needed in order to live now and fell face down. Ulises got away from the lifeless arms and without pausing a moment gave the vast fallen body a final thrust.

Eréndira then put the plate on a table and leaned over her grandmother, scrutinizing her without touching her. When she was convinced that she was dead her face suddenly acquired all the maturity of an older person which her twenty years of misfortune had not given her. With quick and precise movements she grabbed the gold vest and left the tent.

Ulises remained sitting by the corpse, exhausted by the fight, and the more he tried to clean his face the more it was daubed with that green and living matter that seemed to be flowing from his fingers. Only when he saw Eréndira go out with the gold vest did he become aware of his state.

He shouted to her but got no answer. He dragged himself to the entrance to the tent and he saw Eréndira starting to run along the shore away from the city. Then he made a last effort to chase her, calling her with painful shouts that were no longer those of a lover but of a son, yet he was overcome by the terrible drain of having killed a woman without anybody's help. The grandmother's Indians caught up to him lying face down on the beach, weeping from solitude and fear.

Eréndira had not heard him. She was running into the wind, swifter than a deer, and no voice of this world could stop her. Without turning her head she ran past the saltpeter pits, the talcum craters, the torpor of the shacks, until the natural science of the sea ended and the desert began, but she still kept on running with the gold vest beyond the arid winds and the never-ending sunsets and she was never heard of again nor was the slightest trace of her misfortune ever found.

(1972)

The Sea of Lost Time

Toward the end of January the sea was growing harsh, it was beginning to dump its heavy garbage on the town, and a few weeks later everything was contaminated with its unbearable mood. From that time on the world wasn't worth living in, at least until the following December, so no one stayed awake after eight o'clock. But the year Mr. Herbert came the sea didn't change, not even in February. On the contrary, it became smoother and more phosphorescent and during the first nights of March it gave off a fragrance of roses.

Tobías smelled it. His blood attracted crabs and he spent half the night chasing them off his bed until the breeze rose up again and he was able to sleep. During his long moments of lying awake he learned how to distinguish all the changes in the air. So that when he got a smell of roses he didn't have to open up the door to know that it was a smell from the sea.

He got up late. Clotilde was starting a fire in the court-yard. The breeze was cool and all the stars were in place, but it was hard to count them down to the horizon because of the lights from the sea. After having his coffee, Tobías could still taste a trace of night on his palate.

"Something very strange happened last night," he remembered.

Clotilde, of course, had not smelled it. She slept so heavily that she didn't even remember her dreams.

"It was a smell of roses," Tobías said, "and I'm sure it came from the sea."

"I don't know what roses smell like," said Clotilde.

She could have been right. The town was arid, with a hard soil furrowed by saltpeter, and only occasionally did someone bring a bouquet of flowers from outside to cast into the sea where they threw their dead.

"It's the smell that drowned man from Guacamayal had," Tobías said.

"Well," Clotilde said, smiling "if it was a good smell, then you can be sure it didn't come from this sea."

It really was a cruel sea. At certain times, when the nets brought in nothing but floating garbage, the streets of the town were still full of dead fish when the tide went out. Dynamite only brought the remains of old shipwrecks to the surface.

The few women left in town, like Clotilde, were boiling up with bitterness. And like her, there was old Jacob's wife, who got up earlier than usual that morning, put the house in order, and sat down to breakfast with a look of adversity.

"My last wish," she said to her husband, "is to be buried alive."

She said it as if she were on her deathbed, but she was sitting across the table in a dining room with windows through which the bright March light came pouring in and spread throughout the house. Opposite her, calming his peaceful hunger, was old Jacob, a man who had loved her so much and for so long that he could no longer conceive of any suffering that didn't start with his wife.

"I want to die with the assurance that I'll be laid beneath the ground like proper people," she went on. "And the only way to be sure of it is to go around asking people to do me the blessed charity of burying me alive."

"You don't have to ask anybody," old Jacob said with the greatest of calm. "I'll put you there myself."

"Let's go, then," she said, "because I'm going to die before very long."

Old Jacob looked her over carefully. Her eyes were the only thing still young. Her bones had become knotted up at the joints and she had the same look of a plowed field which, when it came right down to it, she had always had.

"You're in better shape than ever," he told her.

"Last night I caught a smell of roses," she sighed.

"Don't pay it any mind," old Jacob said to assure her. "Things like that are always happening to poor people like us."

"Nothing of the sort," she said. "I've always prayed that I'd know enough ahead of time when death would come so I could die far away from this sea. A smell of roses in this town can only be a message from God."

All that old Jacob could think of was to ask for a little time to put things in order. He'd heard tell that people don't die when they ought to but when they want to, and he was seriously worried by his wife's premonition. He even wondered whether, when the moment came, he'd be up to burying her alive.

At nine o'clock he opened the place where he used to have a store. He put two chairs and a small table with the checkerboard on it by the door and he spent all morning playing opponents who happened by. From his house he looked at the ruined town, the shambles of a town with the traces of former colors that had been nibbled away by the sun and a chunk of sea at the end of the street.

Before lunch, as always, he played with Don Máximo Gómez. Old Jacob couldn't imagine a more humane opponent than a man who had survived two civil wars intact and had only sacrificed an eye in the third. After losing one game on purpose, he held him back for another.

"Tell me one thing, Don Máximo," he asked him then. "Would you be capable of burying your wife alive?"

"Certainly," Don Máximo Gómez answered. "You can believe me when I say that my hand wouldn't even tremble."

Old Jacob fell into a surprised silence. Then, after letting himself be despoiled of his best pieces, he sighed:

"Well, the way it looks, Petra is going to die."

Don Máximo Gómez didn't change his expression. "In that case," he said, "there's no reason to bury her alive." He gobbled up two pieces and crowned a king. Then he fastened an eye wet with sad waters on his opponent.

"What's she got?"

"Last night," old Jacob explained, "she caught a smell of roses."

"Then half the town is going to die," Don Máximo

Gómez said. "That's all they've been talking about this morning."

It was hard for old Jacob to lose again without offending him. He brought in the table and the chairs, closed up the shop, and went about everywhere looking for someone who had caught the smell. In the end only Tobías was sure. So he asked him please to stop by his place, as if by chance, and tell his wife all about it.

Tobías did as he was told. At four o'clock, all dressed up in his Sunday best, he appeared on the porch where the wife had spent all afternoon getting old Jacob's widower's outfit together.

He had come up so quietly that the woman was startled.

"Mercy," she exclaimed. "I thought it was the archangel Gabriel."

"Well, you can see it's not," Tobías said. "It's only me and I've come to tell you something."

She adjusted her glasses and went back to work.

"I know what it's all about," she said.

"I bet you don't," Tobías said.

"You caught the smell of roses last night."

"How did you know?" Tobías asked in desolation.

"At my age," the woman said, "there's so much time left over for thinking that a person can become a regular prophet."

Old Jacob, who had his ear pressed against the partition wall in the back of the store, stood up in shame.

"You see, woman," he shouted through the wall. He made a turn and appeared on the porch. "It wasn't what you thought it was after all."

"This boy has been lying," she said without raising her head. "He didn't smell anything."

"It was around eleven o'clock," Tobías said. "I was chasing crabs away."

The woman finished mending a collar.

"Lies," she insisted. "Everybody knows you're a tricker." She bit the thread with her teeth and looked at Tobías over her glasses.

"What I can't understand is why you went to the trouble to put Vaseline on your hair and shine your shoes just to come and be so disrespectful to me."

From then on Tobías began to keep watch on the sea. He hung his hammock up on the porch by the yard and spent the night waiting, surprised by the things that go on in the world while people are asleep. For many nights he could hear the desperate scrawling of the crabs as they tried to claw-climb up the supports of the house, until so many nights went by that they got tired of trying. He came to know Clotilde's way of sleeping. He discovered how her fluty snores became more high-pitched as the heat grew more intense until they became one single languid note in the torpor of July.

At first Tobías kept watch on the sea the way people who know it well do, his gaze fixed on a single point of the horizon. He watched it change color. He watched it turn out its lights and become frothy and dirty and toss up its refuse-laden belches when great rainstorms agitated its digestion. Little by little he learned to keep watch the way people who know it better do, not even looking at it but unable to forget about it even in his sleep.

Old Jacob's wife died in August. She died in her sleep and they had to cast her, like everyone else, into a flowerless sea. Tobías kept on waiting. He had waited so long that it was becoming his way of being. One night, while he was dozing in his hammock, he realized that something in the air had changed. It was an intermittent wave, like the time a Japanese ship had jettisoned a cargo of rotten onions at the harbor mouth. Then the smell thickened and was motionless until dawn. Only when he had the feeling that he could pick it up in his hands and exhibit it did Tobías leap out of his hammock and go into Clotilde's room. He shook her several times.

"Here it is," he told her.

Clotilde had to brush the smell away like a cobweb in order to get up. Then she fell back down on her tepid sheets.

"God curse it," she said.

Tobías leaped toward the door, ran into the middle of the street, and began to shout. He shouted with all his might, took a deep breath and shouted again, and then there was a silence and he took a deeper breath, and the smell was still on the sea. But nobody answered. Then he went about knocking on doors from house to house, even on houses that had no owners, until his uproar got entwined with that of the dogs and he woke everybody up.

Many of them couldn't smell it. But others, especially the old ones, went down to enjoy it on the beach. It was a compact fragrance that left no chink for any odor of the past. Some, worn out from so much smelling, went back to their houses. Most of the people stayed to finish their night's sleep on the beach. By dawn the smell was so pure that it was a pity even to breathe it.

Tobías slept most of the day. Clotilde caught up with him at siesta time and they spent the afternoon frolicking in bed without even closing the door to the yard. First they did it like earthworms, then like rabbits, and finally like turtles, until the world grew sad and it was dark again. There was still a trace of roses in the air. Sometimes a wave of music reached the bedroom.

"It's coming from Catarino's," Clotilde said. "Someone must have come to town."

Three men and a woman had come. Catarino thought that others might come later and he tried to fix his gramophone. Since he couldn't do it, he asked Pancho Aparecido, who did all kinds of things because he'd never owned anything, and besides, he had a box of tools and a pair of intelligent hands.

Catarino's place was a wooden building set apart and facing the sea. It had one large room with benches and small tables, and several bedrooms in the rear. While they watched Pancho Aparecido working, the three men and the woman drank in silence, sitting at the bar and yawning in turn.

The gramophone worked well after several tries. When they heard the music, distant but distinct, the people stopped chatting. They looked at one another and for a moment had nothing to say, for only then did they realize how old they had become since the last time they'd heard music.

Tobías found everybody still awake after nine o'clock. They were sitting in their doorways listening to Catarino's old records, with the same look of childish fatalism of people watching an eclipse. Every record reminded them of someone who had died, the taste of food after a long illness, or something they'd had to do the next day many years ago which never got done because they'd forgotten.

The music stopped around eleven o'clock. Many people went to bed, thinking it was going to rain because a dark cloud hung over the sea. But the cloud descended, floated for a while on the surface, and then sank into the water. Only the stars remained above. A short while later, the breeze went out from the town and came back with a smell of roses.

"Just what I told you, Jacob," Don Máximo Gómez exclaimed. "Here it is back with us again. I'm sure now that we're going to smell it every night."

"God forbid," old Jacob said. "That smell is the only thing in life that's come too late for me."

They'd been playing checkers in the empty store without paying any attention to the records. Their memories were so ancient that there weren't records old enough to stir them up.

"For my part, I don't believe much of anything about this," Don Máximo Gómez said. "After so many years of eating dust, with so many women wanting a little yard to plant flowers in, it's not strange that a person should end up smelling things like this and even thinking it's all true."

"But we can smell it with our own noses," old Jacob said.

"No matter," said Don Máximo Gómez. "During the war, when the revolution was already lost, we'd wanted a general so bad that we saw the Duke of Marlborough appear in flesh and blood. I saw him with my own eyes, Jacob."

It was after midnight. When he was alone, old Jacob closed his store and took his lamp to the bedroom. Through the window, outlined against the glow of the sea, he saw the crag from which they threw their dead.

"Petra," he called in a soft voice.

She couldn't hear him. At that moment she was floating along almost on the surface of the water beneath a radiant noonday sun on the Bay of Bengal. She'd lifted her head

to look through the water, as through an illuminated show-
case, at a huge ocean liner. But she couldn't see her husband, who at that moment on the other side of the world
was starting to hear Catarino's gramophone again.

"Just think," old Jacob said. "Barely six months ago they
thought you were crazy and now they're the ones making
a festival out of the smell that brought on your death."

He put out the light and got into bed. He wept slowly
with that graceless little whimper old people have, but soon
he fell asleep.

"I'd get away from this town if I could," he sobbed as he
tossed. "I'd go straight to hell or anywhere else if I could
only get twenty pesos together."

From that night on and for several weeks, the smell remained on the sea. It impregnated the wood of the houses,
the food, and the drinking water, and there was nowhere
to escape the odor. A lot of people were startled to find it
in the vapors of their own shit. The men and the women
who had come to Catarino's place left one Friday, but they
were back on Saturday with a whole mob. More people
arrived on Sunday. They were in and out of everywhere like
ants, looking for something to eat and a place to sleep, until
it got to be impossible to walk the streets.

More people came. The women who had left when the
town died came back to Catarino's. They were fatter and
wore heavier make-up, and they brought the latest records,
which didn't remind anyone of anything. Some of the former inhabitants of the town returned. They'd gone off to
get filthy rich somewhere else and they came back talking
about their fortunes but wearing the same clothes they'd
left with. Music and side shows arrived, wheels of chance,
fortunetellers and gunmen and men with snakes coiled

about their necks who were selling the elixir of eternal life.
They kept on coming for many weeks, even after the first
rains had come and the sea became rough and the smell
disappeared.

A priest arrived among the last. He walked all over, eating bread dipped in light coffee, and little by little, he
banned everything that had come before him: games of
chance, the new music and the way it was danced, and even
the recent custom of sleeping on the beach. One evening,
at Melchor's house, he preached a sermon about the smell
of the sea.

"Give thanks to heaven, my children," he said, "for this
is the smell of God."

Someone interrupted him.

"How can you tell, Father? You haven't smelled it yet."

"The Holy Scriptures," he said, "are quite explicit in
regard to this smell. We are living in a chosen village."

Tobías went about back and forth in the festival like a
sleepwalker. He took Clotilde to see what money was. They
made believe they were betting enormous sums at roulette,
and then they figured things up and felt extremely rich with
all the money they could have won. But one night not just
they, the whole multitude occupying the town, saw more
money in one place than they could possibly have imagined.

That was the night Mr. Herbert arrived. He appeared
suddenly, set up a table in the middle of the street, and on
top of the table placed two large trunks brimful with bank
notes. There was so much money that no one noticed it at
first, because they couldn't believe it was true. But when
Mr. Herbert started ringing a little bell, the people had to

believe him, and they went over to listen.

"I'm the richest man in the world," he said. "I've got so much money I haven't got room to keep it any more. And besides, since my heart's so big that there's no room for it in my chest, I have decided to travel the world over solving the problems of mankind."

He was tall and ruddy. He spoke in a loud voice and without any pauses, and simultaneously he waved about a pair of lukewarm, languid hands that always looked as if they'd just been shaved. He spoke for fifteen minutes and rested. Then he rang the little bell and began to speak again. Halfway through his speech, someone in the crowd waved a hat and interrupted him.

"Come on, mister, don't talk so much and start handing out the money."

"Not so fast," Mr. Herbert replied. "Handing out money with no rhyme or reason, in addition to being an unfair way of doing things, doesn't make any sense at all."

With his eyes he located the man who had interrupted him, and motioned him to come forward. The crowd let him through.

"On the other hand," Mr. Herbert went on, "this impatient friend of ours is going to give us a chance to explain the most equitable system of the distribution of wealth." He reached out a hand and helped him up.

"What's your name?"

"Patricio."

"All right, Patricio," Mr. Herbert said. "Just like everybody else, you've got some problem you haven't been able to solve for some time."

Patricio took off his hat and confirmed it with a nod.

"What is it?"

"Well, my problem is this," Patricio said. "I haven't got any money."

"How much do you need?"

"Forty-eight pesos."

Mr. Herbert gave an exclamation of triumph. "Forty-eight pesos," he repeated. The crowd accompanied him in clapping.

"Very well, Patricio," Mr. Herbert went on. "Now, tell us one thing: what can you do?"

"Lots of things."

"Decide on one," Mr. Herbert said. "The thing you do best."

"Well," Patricio said, "I can do birds."

Applauding a second time, Mr. Herbert turned to the crowd.

"So, then, ladies and gentlemen, our friend Patricio, who does an extraordinary job at imitating birds, is going to imitate forty-eight different birds and in that way he will solve the great problem of his life."

To the startled silence of the crowd, Patricio then did his birds. Sometimes whistling, sometimes with his throat, he did all known birds and finished off the figure with others that no one was able to identify. When he was through, Mr. Herbert called for a round of applause and gave him forty-eight pesos.

"And now," he said, "come up one by one. I'm going to be here until tomorrow at this time solving problems."

Old Jacob learned about the commotion from the comments of people walking past his house. With each bit of news his heart grew bigger and bigger until he felt it burst.

"What do you think about this gringo?" he asked.

Don Máximo Gómez shrugged his shoulders. "He must be a philanthropist."

"If I could only do something," old Jacob said, "I could solve my little problem right now. It's nothing much: twenty pesos."

"You play a good game of checkers," Don Máximo Gómez said.

Old Jacob appeared not to have paid any attention to him, but when he was alone, he wrapped up the board and the box of checkers in a newspaper and went off to challenge Mr. Herbert. He waited until midnight for his turn. Finally Mr. Herbert had them pack up his trunks and said good-bye until the next morning.

He didn't go off to bed. He showed up at Catarino's place with the men who were carrying his trunks and the crowd followed him all the way there with their problems. Little by little, he went on solving them, and he solved so many that finally, in the store, the only ones left were the women and some men with their problems already solved. And in the back of the room there was a solitary woman fanning herself slowly with a cardboard advertisement.

"What about you?" Mr. Herbert shouted at her. "What's your problem?"

The woman stopped fanning herself.

"Don't try to get me mixed up in your fun, mister gringo," she shouted across the room. "I haven't got any kind of problem and I'm a whore because it comes out of my balls."

Mr. Herbert shrugged his shoulders. He went on drinking his cold beer beside the open trunks, waiting for other problems. He was sweating. A while later, a woman broke away from the group that was with her at the table and spoke to him in a low voice. She had a five-hundred-peso problem.

"How would you split that up?" Mr. Herbert asked her.

"By five."

"Just imagine," Mr. Herbert said. "That's a hundred men."

"It doesn't matter," she said. "If I can get all that money together they'll be the last hundred men of my life."

He looked her over. She was quite young, fragile-boned, but her eyes showed a simple decision.

"All right," Mr. Herbert said. "Go into your room and I'll start sending each one with his five pesos to you."

He went to the street door and rang his little bell.

At seven o'clock in the morning Tobías found Catarino's place open. All the lights were out. Half asleep and puffed up with beer, Mr. Herbert was controlling the entry of men into the girl's room.

Tobías went in too. The girl recognized him and was surprised to see him in her room.

"You too?"

"They told me to come in," Tobías said. "They gave me five pesos and told me not to take too long."

She took the soaked sheet off the bed and asked Tobías to hold the other end. It was as heavy as canvas. They squeezed it, twisting it by the ends, until it got its natural weight back. They turned the mattress over and the sweat came out the other side. Tobías did things as best he could. Before leaving he put the five pesos on the pile of bills that was growing high beside the bed.

"Send everybody you can," Mr. Herbert suggested to him. "Let's see if we can get this over with before noon."

The girl opened the door a crack and asked for a cold beer. There were still several men waiting.

"How many left?" she asked.

"Sixty-three," Mr. Herbert answered.

Old Jacob followed him about all day with his checkerboard. His turn came at nightfall and he laid out his problem and Mr. Herbert accepted. They put two chairs and a small table on top of the big table in the middle of the street, and old Jacob made the first move. It was the last play he was able to premeditate. He lost.

"Forty pesos," Mr. Herbert said, "and I'll give you a handicap of two moves."

He won again. His hands barely touched the checkers. He played blindfolded, guessing his opponent's moves, and still won. The crowd grew tired of watching. When old Jacob decided to give up, he was in debt to the tune of five thousand seven hundred forty-two pesos and twenty-three cents.

He didn't change his expression. He jotted down the figure on a piece of paper he had in his pocket. Then he folded up the board, put the checkers in their box, and wrapped everything in the newspaper.

"Do with me what you will," he said, "but let me have these things. I promise you that I will spend the rest of my life getting all that money together."

Mr. Herbert looked at his watch.

"I'm terribly sorry," he said. "Your time will be up in twenty minutes." He waited until he was sure that his opponent hadn't found the solution. "Don't you have anything else to offer?"

"My honor."

"I mean," Mr. Herbert explained, "something that changes color when a brush daubed with paint is passed over it."

"My house," old Jacob said as if he were solving a riddle. "It's not worth much, but it is a house."

That was how Mr. Herbert took possession of old Jacob's house. He also took possession of the houses and property of others who couldn't pay their debts, but he called for a week of music, fireworks, and acrobats and he took charge of the festivities himself.

It was a memorable week. Mr. Herbert spoke of the miraculous destiny of the town and he even sketched out the city of the future, great glass buildings with dance floors on top. He showed it to the crowd. They looked in astonishment, trying to find themselves among the pedestrians painted in Mr. Herbert's colors, but they were so well dressed that they couldn't recognize themselves. It pained them to be using him so much. They laughed at the urge they'd had to cry back in October and they kept on living in the mist of hope until Mr. Herbert rang his little bell and said the party was over. Only then did he get some rest.

"You're going to die from that life you lead," old Jacob said.

"I've got so much money that there's no reason for me to die," Mr. Herbert said.

He flopped onto his bed. He slept for days on end, snoring like a lion, and so many days went by that people grew tired of waiting on him. They had to dig crabs to eat. Catarino's new records got so old that no one could listen to them any more without tears, and he had to close his place up.

A long time after Mr. Herbert had fallen asleep, the

priest knocked on old Jacob's door. The house was locked from the inside. As the breathing of the man asleep had been using up the air, things had lost their weight and were beginning to float about.

"I want to have a word with him," the priest said.

"You'll have to wait," said old Jacob.

"I haven't got much time."

"Have a seat, Father, and wait," old Jacob repeated. "And please talk to me in the meantime. It's been a long time since I've known what's been going on in the world."

"People have all scattered," the priest said. "It won't be long before the town will be the same as it was before. That's the only thing that's new."

"They'll come back when the sea smells of roses again," old Jacob said.

"But meanwhile, we've got to sustain the illusions of those who stay with something," the priest said. "It's urgent that we start building the church."

"That's why you've come to see Mr. Herbert," old Jacob said.

"That's right," said the priest. "Gringos are very charitable."

"Wait a bit, then, Father," old Jacob said. "He might just wake up."

They played checkers. It was a long and difficult game which lasted several days, but Mr. Herbert didn't wake up.

The priest let himself be confused by desperation. He went all over with a copper plate asking for donations to build the church, but he didn't get very much. He was getting more and more diaphanous from so much begging, his bones were starting to fill with sounds, and one Sunday he rose two hands above the ground, but nobody noticed it. Then he packed his clothes in one suitcase and the money he had collected in another and said good-bye forever.

"The smell won't come back," he said to those who tried to dissuade him. "You've got to face up to the fact that the town has fallen into mortal sin."

When Mr. Herbert woke up the town was the same as it had been before. The rain had fermented the garbage the crowds had left in the streets and the soil was as arid and hard as a brick once more.

"I've been asleep a long time," Mr. Herbert said, yawning.

"Centuries," said old Jacob.

"I'm starving to death."

"So is everybody else," old Jacob said. "There's nothing to do but go to the beach and dig for crabs."

Tobías found him scratching in the sand, foaming at the mouth, and he was surprised to discover that when rich people were starving they looked so much like the poor. Mr. Herbert didn't find enough crabs. At nightfall he invited Tobías to come look for something to eat in the depths of the sea.

"Listen," Tobías warned him, "only the dead know what's down inside there."

"Scientists know too," Mr. Herbert said. "Beneath the sea of the drowned there are turtles with exquisite meat on them. Get your clothes off and let's go."

They went. At first they swam straight along and then down very deep to where the light of the sun stopped and then the light of the sea, and things were visible only in their own light. They passed by a submerged village with men and women on horseback turning about a musical kiosk. It was a splendid day and there were brightly colored flowers on the terraces.

"A Sunday sank at about eleven o'clock in the morning," Mr. Herbert said. "It must have been some cataclysm."

Tobías turned off toward the village, but Mr. Herbert signaled him to keep going down.

"There are roses there," Tobías said. "I want Clotilde to know what they are."

"You can come back another time at your leisure," Mr. Herbert said. "Right now I'm dying of hunger."

He went down like an octopus, with slow, slinky strokes of his arms. Tobías, who was trying hard not to lose sight of him, thought that it must be the way rich people swam. Little by little, they were leaving the sea of common catastrophes and entering the sea of the dead.

There were so many of them that Tobías thought that he'd never seen as many people on earth. They were floating motionless, face up, on different levels, and they all had the look of forgotten souls.

"They're very old dead," Mr. Herbert said. "It's taken them centuries to reach this state of repose."

Farther down, in the waters of the more recent dead, Mr. Herbert stopped. Tobías caught up with him at the instant that a very young woman passed in front of them. She was floating on her side, her eyes open, followed by a current of flowers.

Mr. Herbert put his finger to his lip and held it there until the last of the flowers went by.

"She's the most beautiful woman I've ever seen in all my life," he said.

"She's old Jacob's wife," Tobías said. "She must be fifty years younger, but that's her. I'm sure of it."

"She's done a lot of traveling," Mr. Herbert said. "She's carrying behind her flowers from all the seas of the world."

They reached bottom. Mr. Herbert took a few turns over earth that looked like polished slate. Tobías followed him. Only when he became accustomed to the half light of the depths did he discover that the turtles were there. There were thousands of them, flattened out on the bottom, so motionless they looked petrified.

"They're alive," Mr. Herbert said, "but they've been asleep for millions of years."

He turned one over. With a soft touch he pushed it upward and the sleeping animal left his hands and continued drifting up. Tobías let it pass by. Then he looked toward the surface and saw the whole sea upside down.

"It's like a dream," he said.

"For your own good," Mr. Herbert said, "don't tell anyone about it. Just imagine the disorder there'd be in the world if people found out about these things."

It was almost midnight when they got back to the village. They woke up Clotilde to boil some water. Mr. Herbert butchered the turtle, but it took all three of them to chase and kill the heart a second time as it bounced out into the courtyard while they were cutting the creature up. They ate until they couldn't breathe any more.

"Well, Tobías," Mr. Herbert then said, "we've got to face reality."

"Of course."

"And reality says," Mr. Herbert went on, "that the smell will never come back."

"It will come back."

"It won't come back," Clotilde put in, "among other

reasons because it never really came. It was you who got everybody all worked up."

"You smelled it yourself," Tobías said.

"I was half dazed that night," Clotilde said. "But right now I'm not sure about anything that has to do with this sea."

"So I'll be on my way," Mr. Herbert said. "And," he added, speaking to both of them, "you should leave too. There are too many things to do in the world for you to be starving in this town."

He left. Tobías stayed in the yard counting the stars down to the horizon and he discovered that there were three more since last December. Clotilde called him from the bedroom, but he didn't pay any attention.

"Come here, you dummy," Clotilde insisted. "It's been years since we did it like rabbits."

Tobías waited a long time. When he finally went in, she had fallen asleep. He half woke her, but she was so tired that they both got things mixed up and they were only able to do it like earthworms.

"You're acting like a boob," Clotilde said grouchily. "Try to think about something else."

"I am thinking about something else."

She wanted to know what it was and he decided to tell her on the condition that she wouldn't repeat it. Clotilde promised.

"There's a village at the bottom of the sea," Tobías said, "with little white houses with millions of flowers on the terraces."

Clotilde raised her hands to her head.

"Oh, Tobías," she exclaimed. "Oh, Tobías, for the love

of God, don't start up with those things again."

Tobías didn't say anything else. He rolled over to the edge of the bed and tried to go to sleep. He couldn't until dawn, when the wind changed and the crabs left him in peace.

(1961)

Death Constant Beyond Love

SENATOR ONÉSIMO SÁNCHEZ had six months and eleven days to go before his death when he found the woman of his life. He met her in Rosal del Virrey, an illusory village which by night was the furtive wharf for smugglers' ships, and on the other hand, in broad daylight looked like the most useless inlet on the desert, facing a sea that was arid and without direction and so far from everything no one would have suspected that someone capable of changing the destiny of anyone lived there. Even its name was a kind of joke, because the only rose in that village was being worn by Senator Onésimo Sánchez himself on the same afternoon when he met Laura Farina.

It was an unavoidable stop in the electoral campaign he made every four years. The carnival wagons had arrived in the morning. Then came the trucks with the rented Indians who were carried into the towns in order to enlarge the crowds at public ceremonies. A short time before eleven o'clock, along with the music and rockets and jeeps of the retinue, the ministerial automobile, the color of strawberry soda, arrived. Senator Onésimo Sánchez was placid and weatherless inside the air-conditioned car, but as soon as he opened the door he was shaken by a gust of fire and his shirt of pure silk was soaked in a kind of light-colored soup and he felt many years older and more alone than ever. In real life he had just turned forty-two, had been graduated from Göttingen with honors as a metallurgical engineer, and was an avid reader, although without much reward, of badly translated Latin classics. He was married to a radiant German woman who had given him five children and they were all happy in their home, he the happiest of all until they told him, three months before, that he would be dead forever by next Christmas.

While the preparations for the public rally were being completed, the senator managed to have an hour alone in the house they had set aside for him to rest in. Before he lay down he put in a glass of drinking water the rose he had kept alive all across the desert, lunched on the diet cereals that he took with him so as to avoid the repeated portions of fried goat that were waiting for him during the rest of the day, and he took several analgesic pills before the time prescribed so that he would have the remedy ahead of the pain. Then he put the electric fan close to the hammock and stretched out naked for fifteen minutes in the shadow of the rose, making a great effort at mental distraction so as not to think about death while he dozed. Except for the doctors, no one knew that he had been sentenced to a fixed term, for he had decided to endure his secret all alone, with no change in his life, not because of pride but out of shame.

He felt in full control of his will when he appeared in public again at three in the afternoon, rested and clean, wearing a pair of coarse linen slacks and a floral shirt, and with his soul sustained by the anti-pain pills. Nevertheless, the erosion of death was much more pernicious than he had supposed, for as he went up onto the platform he felt a strange disdain for those who were fighting for the good luck to shake his hand, and he didn't feel sorry as he had at other times for the groups of barefoot Indians who could scarcely bear the hot saltpeter coals of the sterile little square. He silenced the applause with a wave of his hand, almost with rage, and he began to speak without gestures, his eyes fixed on the sea, which was sighing with heat. His measured, deep voice had the quality of calm water, but the speech that had been memorized and ground out so many times had not occurred to him in the nature of telling the truth, but, rather, as the opposite of a fatalistic pronouncement by Marcus Aurelius in the fourth book of his *Meditations.*

"We are here for the purpose of defeating nature," he began, against all his convictions. "We will no longer be foundlings in our own country, orphans of God in a realm of thirst and bad climate, exiles in our own land. We will be different people, ladies and gentlemen, we will be a great and happy people."

There was a pattern to his circus. As he spoke his aides threw clusters of paper birds into the air and the artificial creatures took on life, flew about the platform of planks, and went out to sea. At the same time, other men took some prop trees with felt leaves out of the wagons and planted them in the saltpeter soil behind the crowd. They finished by setting up a cardboard façade with make-believe houses of red brick that had glass windows, and with it they covered the miserable real-life shacks.

The senator prolonged his speech with two quotations in Latin in order to give the farce more time. He promised rainmaking machines, portable breeders for table animals, the oils of happiness which would make vegetables grow in the saltpeter and clumps of pansies in the window boxes. When he saw that his fictional world was all set up, he pointed to it. "That's the way it will be for us, ladies and gentlemen," he shouted. "Look! That's the way it will be for us."

The audience turned around. An ocean liner made of painted paper was passing behind the houses and it was taller than the tallest houses in the artificial city. Only the senator himself noticed that since it had been set up and taken down and carried from one place to another the superimposed cardboard town had been eaten away by the terrible climate and that it was almost as poor and dusty as Rosal del Virrey.

For the first time in twelve years, Nelson Farina didn't go to greet the senator. He listened to the speech from his hammock amidst the remains of his siesta, under the cool bower of a house of unplaned boards which he had built with the same pharmacist's hands with which he had drawn and quartered his first wife. He had escaped from Devil's Island and appeared in Rosal del Virrey on a ship loaded with innocent macaws, with a beautiful and blasphemous black woman he had found in Paramaribo and by whom he had a daughter. The woman died of natural causes a short while later and she didn't suffer the fate of the other, whose pieces had fertilized her own cauliflower patch, but was buried whole and with her Dutch name in the local cemetery. The daughter had inherited her color and her figure along with her father's yellow and astonished eyes, and he had good reason to imagine that he was rearing the most beautiful woman in the world.

Ever since he had met Senator Onésimo Sánchez during his first electoral campaign, Nelson Farina had begged for his help in getting a false identity card which would place him beyond the reach of the law. The senator, in a friendly but firm way, had refused. Nelson Farina never gave up, and for several years, every time he found the chance, he would repeat his request with a different recourse. But this time he stayed in his hammock, condemned to rot alive in that burning den of buccaneers. When he heard the final applause, he lifted his head, and looking over the boards of the fence, he saw the back side of the farce: the props for the buildings, the framework of the trees, the hidden illusionists who were pushing the ocean liner along. He spat without rancor.

"Merde," he said. *"C'est le Blacamén de la politique."*

After the speech, as was customary, the senator took a walk through the streets of the town in the midst of the music and the rockets and was besieged by the townspeople, who told him their troubles. The senator listened to them good-naturedly and he always found some way to console everybody without having to do them any difficult favors. A woman up on the roof of a house with her six youngest children managed to make herself heard over the uproar and the fireworks.

"I'm not asking for much, Senator," she said. "Just a donkey to haul water from Hanged Man's Well."

The senator noticed the six thin children. "What became of your husband?" he asked.

"He went to find his fortune on the island of Aruba," the woman answered good-humoredly, "and what he found was a foreign woman, the kind that put diamonds on their teeth."

The answer brought on a roar of laughter.

"All right," the senator decided, "you'll get your donkey."

A short while later an aide of his brought a good pack donkey to the woman's house and on the rump it had a campaign slogan written in indelible paint so that no one would ever forget that it was a gift from the senator.

Along the short stretch of street he made other, smaller gestures, and he even gave a spoonful of medicine to a sick man who had had his bed brought to the door of his house so he could see him pass. At the last corner, through the boards of the fence, he saw Nelson Farina in his hammock, looking ashen and gloomy, but nonetheless the senator greeted him, with no show of affection.

"Hello, how are you?"

Nelson Farina turned in his hammock and soaked him in the sad amber of his look.

"Moi, vous savez," he said.

His daughter came out into the yard when she heard the greeting. She was wearing a cheap, faded Guajiro Indian robe, her head was decorated with colored bows, and her face was painted as protection against the sun, but even in that state of disrepair it was possible to imagine that there had never been another so beautiful in the whole world. The senator was left breathless. "I'll be damned!" he breathed in surprise. "The Lord does the craziest things!"

That night Nelson Farina dressed his daughter up in her best clothes and sent her to the senator. Two guards armed with rifles who were nodding from the heat in the borrowed house ordered her to wait on the only chair in the vestibule.

The senator was in the next room meeting with the important people of Rosal del Virrey, whom he had gathered together in order to sing for them the truths he had left out of his speeches. They looked so much like all the ones he always met in all the towns in the desert that even the senator himself was sick and tired of that perpetual nightly session. His shirt was soaked with sweat and he was trying to dry it on his body with the hot breeze from an electric fan that was buzzing like a horse fly in the heavy heat of the room.

"We, of course, can't eat paper birds," he said. "You and I know that the day there are trees and flowers in this heap of goat dung, the day there are shad instead of worms in the water holes, that day neither you nor I will have anything to do here, do I make myself clear?"

No one answered. While he was speaking, the senator had torn a sheet off the calendar and fashioned a paper butterfly out of it with his hands. He tossed it with no particular aim into the air current coming from the fan and the butterfly flew about the room and then went out through the half-open door. The senator went on speaking with a control aided by the complicity of death.

"Therefore," he said, "I don't have to repeat to you what you already know too well: that my reelection is a better piece of business for you than it is for me, because I'm fed up with stagnant water and Indian sweat, while you people, on the other hand, make your living from it."

Laura Farina saw the paper butterfly come out. Only she

saw it because the guards in the vestibule had fallen asleep on the steps, hugging their rifles. After a few turns, the large lithographed butterfly unfolded completely, flattened against the wall, and remained stuck there. Laura Farina tried to pull it off with her nails. One of the guards, who woke up with the applause from the next room, noticed her vain attempt.

"It won't come off," he said sleepily. "It's painted on the wall."

Laura Farina sat down again when the men began to come out of the meeting. The senator stood in the doorway of the room with his hand on the latch, and he only noticed Laura Farina when the vestibule was empty.

"What are you doing here?"

"C'est de la part de mon père," she said.

The senator understood. He scrutinized the sleeping guards, then he scrutinized Laura Farina, whose unusual beauty was even more demanding than his pain, and he resolved then that death had made his decision for him.

"Come in," he told her.

Laura Farina was struck dumb standing in the doorway to the room: thousands of bank notes were floating in the air, flapping like the butterfly. But the senator turned off the fan and the bills were left without air and alighted on the objects in the room.

"You see," he said, smiling, "even shit can fly."

Laura Farina sat down on a schoolboy's stool. Her skin was smooth and firm, with the same color and the same solar density as crude oil, her hair was the mane of a young mare, and her huge eyes were brighter than the light. The senator followed the thread of her look and finally found the rose, which had been tarnished by the saltpeter.

"It's a rose," he said.

"Yes," she said with a trace of perplexity. "I learned what they were in Riohacha."

The senator sat down on an army cot, talking about roses as he unbuttoned his shirt. On the side where he imagined his heart to be inside his chest he had a corsair's tattoo of a heart pierced by an arrow. He threw the soaked shirt to the floor and asked Laura Farina to help him off with his boots.

She knelt down facing the cot. The senator continued to scrutinize her, thoughtfully, and while she was untying the laces he wondered which one of them would end up with the bad luck of that encounter.

"You're just a child," he said.

"Don't you believe it," she said. "I'll be nineteen in April."

The senator became interested.

"What day?"

"The eleventh," she said.

The senator felt better. "We're both Aries," he said. And smiling, he added:

"It's the sign of solitude."

Laura Farina wasn't paying attention because she didn't know what to do with the boots. The senator, for his part, didn't know what to do with Laura Farina, because he wasn't used to sudden love affairs and, besides, he knew that the one at hand had its origins in indignity. Just to have some time to think, he held Laura Farina tightly between his knees, embraced her about the waist, and lay down on his back on the cot. Then he realized that she was naked under her dress, for her body gave off the dark fragrance of an animal of the woods, but her heart was frightened and her skin disturbed by a glacial sweat.

"No one loves us," he sighed.

Laura Farina tried to say something, but there was only enough air for her to breathe. He laid her down beside him to help her, he put out the light and the room was in the shadow of the rose. She abandoned herself to the mercies of her fate. The senator caressed her slowly, seeking her with his hand, barely touching her, but where he expected to find her, he came across something iron that was in the way.

"What have you got there?"

"A padlock," she said.

"What in hell!" the senator said furiously and asked what he knew only too well. "Where's the key?"

Laura Farina gave a breath of relief.

"My papa has it," she answered. "He told me to tell you to send one of your people to get it and to send along with him a written promise that you'll straighten out his situation."

The senator grew tense. "Frog bastard," he murmured indignantly. Then he closed his eyes in order to relax and he met himself in the darkness. *Remember,* he remembered, *that whether it's you or someone else, it won't be long before you'll be dead and it won't be long before your name won't even be left.*

He waited for the shudder to pass.

"Tell me one thing," he asked then. "What have you heard about me?"

"Do you want the honest-to-God truth?"

"The honest-to-God truth."

"Well," Laura Farina ventured, "they say you're worse than the rest because you're different."

The senator didn't get upset. He remained silent for a long time with his eyes closed, and when he opened them again he seemed to have returned from his most hidden instincts.

"Oh, what the hell," he decided. "Tell your son of a bitch of a father that I'll straighten out his situation."

"If you want, I can go get the key myself," Laura Farina said.

The senator held her back.

"Forget about the key," he said, "and sleep awhile with me. It's good to be with someone when you're so alone."

Then she laid his head on her shoulder with her eyes fixed on the rose. The senator held her about the waist, sank his face into woods-animal armpit, and gave in to terror. Six months and eleven days later he would die in that same position, debased and repudiated because of the public scandal with Laura Farina and weeping with rage at dying without her.

(1970)

The Third Resignation

THERE WAS THAT NOISE AGAIN. That cold, cutting, vertical noise that he knew so well now; but it was coming to him now sharp and painful, as if he had become unaccustomed to it overnight.

It was spinning around inside his empty head, dull and biting. A beehive had risen up inside the four walls of his skull. It grew larger and larger with successive spirals, and it beat on him inside, making the stem of his spinal cord quiver with an irregular vibration, out of pitch with the sure rhythm of his body. Something had become unadapted in his human material structure; something that had functioned normally "at other times" and now was hammering at his head from within with dry and hard blows made by the bones of a fleshless, skeletal hand, and it made him remember all the bitter sensations of life. He had the animal impulse to clench his fists and squeeze his temples, which sprouted blue and purple arteries with the firm pressure of his desperate pain. He would have liked to catch the noise that was piercing the moment with its sharp diamond point between the palms of his sensitive hands. The figure of a domestic cat made his muscles contract when he imagined it chasing through the tormented corners of his hot, fever-torn head. Now he would catch it. No. The noise had slippery fur, almost untouchable. But he was ready to catch it with his well-learned strategy and hold it long and tightly with all the strength of his desperation. He would not permit it to enter through his ear again, to come out through his mouth, through each one of his pores or his eyes, which rolled as it went through and remained blind, looking at the flight of the noise from the depths of the shattered darkness. He would not allow it to break its cut-glass crystals, its ice stars, against the interior wall of his cranium. That was what that noise was like: interminable, like a child beating his head against a concrete wall. Like all hard blows against nature's firm things. But if he could encircle it, isolate it, it would no longer torment him. Go and cut the variable figure from its own shadow. Grab it. Squeeze it, yes, once and for all now. Throw it onto the pavement with all his might and step on it ferociously until he could say, panting, that he had killed the noise that was tormenting him, that was driving him mad, and that was now stretched out on the ground like any ordinary thing, transformed into an integral death.

But it was impossible for him to squeeze his temples. His arms had been shortened on him and were now the limbs of a dwarf; small, chubby, adipose arms. He tried to shake his head. He shook it. The noise then appeared with greater force inside his skull, which had hardened, grown larger, felt itself more strongly attracted by gravity. The noise was heavy and hard. So heavy and hard that once he had caught and destroyed it, he would have the impression that he had plucked the petals off a lead flower.

He had heard the noise with the same insistence "at other times." He had heard it, for instance, on the day he had died for the first time. The time—when he saw a corpse —that he realized it was his own corpse. He looked at it and he touched it. He felt himself untouchable, unspatial, nonexistent. He really was a corpse and he could already feel the passage of death on his young and sickly body. The atmosphere had hardened all through the house, as if it had been filled with cement, and in the middle of that block— where objects had remained as when it had been an atmosphere of air—there he was, carefully placed inside a coffin of hard but transparent cement. "That noise" had been in his head that time too. How distant and how cold the soles of his feet had felt there at the other end of the coffin, where they had placed a pillow, because the box was still too big for him and they had to adjust it, adapt the dead body to its new and last garment. They covered him with white and tied a handkerchief around his jaw; mortally handsome.

He was in his coffin, ready to be buried, and yet he knew that he wasn't dead. That if he tried to get up he could do it so easily. "Spiritually," at least. But it wasn't worth the trouble. Better to let himself die right there; die of "death," which was his illness. It had been some time since the doctor had said to his mother dryly:

"Madam, your child has a grave illness: he is dead. Nevertheless," he went on, "we shall do everything possible to keep him alive beyond death. We will succeed in making his organic functions continue through a complex system of autonutrition. Only the motor functions will be different, his spontaneous movements. We shall watch his life through growth, which, too, shall continue on in a normal fashion. It is simply 'a living death.' A real and true death . . ."

He remembered the words but in a confused way. Perhaps he had never heard them and it was the creation of his brain as his temperature rose during the crisis of typhoid fever.

While he was sinking into delirium. When he had read the tales of embalmed pharaohs. As his fever rose, he felt himself to be the protagonist. A kind of emptiness in his life had begun there. From then on he had been unable to distinguish, to remember what events were part of his delirium and what were part of his real life. That was why he doubted now. Perhaps the doctor had never mentioned that strange "living death." It was illogical, paradoxical, simply contradictory. And it made him suspect now that he really was dead. That he had been for eighteen years.

It was then—at the time of his death when he was seven years old—that his mother had had a small coffin made for him out of green wood; a child's coffin, but the doctor had ordered them to make a larger box, a box for a normal adult, because that one there might atrophy growth and he would develop into a deformed dead person or an abnormal living one. Or the detention of growth might impede his realizing that he was getting better. In view of that warning, his mother had a large coffin made for him, one for an adult corpse, and in it she placed three pillows at his feet so that he would fit it properly.

Soon he began to grow inside the box in such a way that every year they would remove some wool from the end pillow so as to give him room for growth. That was how he had spent half his life. Eighteen years. (He was twenty-five now.) And he had reached his normal, definitive height. The carpenter and the doctor had been mistaken in their calculations and had made the coffin two feet too long. They had thought he would have the stature of his father, who had been a half-savage giant. But that was not how it was. The only thing he had inherited from him was his thick beard. A thick, blue beard, which his mother was in the habit of arranging so as to give him a more decent appearance in his coffin. That beard bothered him terribly on hot days.

But there was something that worried him more than "the noise!" It was the mice. Even as a child nothing in the world had worried him more, had produced more terror in him than mice. And it was precisely those disgusting animals who had been attracted by the smell of the candles that burned at his feet. They had already gnawed his clothes and he knew that soon they would start gnawing him, eating his body. One day he was able to see them: they were five shiny, slithery mice who had climbed up into the box by the table leg and were devouring him. By the time his mother noticed it there would be nothing left of him except rubble, his hard, cold bones. What produced even more horror in him was not exactly that the mice would eat him. After all, he could go on living with his skeleton. What tormented him was the innate terror he felt toward those small animals. His hair stood on end just thinking about those velvety creatures who ran all over his body, got into the folds of his skin, and brushed his lips with their icy paws. One of them climbed up to his eyelids and tried to gnaw at his cornea. He saw it, large and monstrous, in its desperate effort to bore through his retina. He thought that it was a new death and surrendered completely to the imminence of vertigo.

He remembered that he had reached adulthood. He was twenty-five years old and that meant that he wouldn't grow any more. His features would become firm, serious. But when he was healthy he wouldn't be able to talk about his childhood. He hadn't had any. He had spent it dead.

His mother had taken rigorous care during the time between childhood and puberty. She was concerned about the perfect hygiene of the coffin and the room as a whole. She changed the flowers in the vases frequently and opened the windows every day so that the fresh air could come in. It was with great satisfaction that she examined the metric tape in those days, when after measuring him she would ascertain that he had grown several centimeters. She had the maternal satisfaction of seeing him alive. Still, she took care to avoid the presence of strangers in the house. After all, the existence of a corpse in family quarters over long years was disagreeable and mysterious. She was a woman of abnegation. But soon her optimism began to decline. During the last years, he saw her look at the metric tape with sadness. Her child was no longer growing. For the past few months the growth had not progressed a single millimeter. His mother knew that now it would be difficult to observe the presence of life in her beloved corpse. She had the fear that one morning she would find him "really" dead, and perhaps because of that on the day in question he was able to observe that she approached his box discreetly and smelled his body. She had fallen into a crisis of pessimism. Of late she had neglected her attentions and no longer took the precaution of carrying the metric tape. She knew that he wasn't going to grow any more.

And he knew that now he was "really" dead. He knew it because of that gentle tranquillity with which his organism had let itself be carried off. Everything had changed unseasonably. The imperceptible beats that only he could perceive had disappeared from his pulse now. He felt heavy, drawn by a reclaiming and potent force toward the primitive substance of the earth. The force of gravity seemed to attract him now with an irrevocable power. He was heavy, like a positive, undeniable corpse. But it was more restful that way. He didn't even have to breathe in order to live his death.

In an imaginary way, without touching himself, one by one he went over his members. There, on a hard pillow, was his head, turned a bit toward the left. He imagined his mouth slightly open because of the narrow strip of cold that filled his throat with hail. He had been chopped down like a twenty-five-year-old tree. Perhaps he had tried to close his mouth. The handkerchief that had held his jaw was loose. He was unable to get himself in place, compose himself, even to strike a pose to look like a decent corpse. His muscles, his members no longer responded as before, punctual to the call of the nervous system. He was no longer what he had been eighteen years before, a normal child who could move as he wished. He felt his fallen arms, fallen forever, tight against the cushioned sides of the coffin. His stomach hard, like the bark of a walnut tree. And beyond there were his legs, whole, exact, completing his perfect adult anatomy. His body rested heavily, but peacefully, with no discomfort whatever, as if the world had suddenly stopped and no one would break the silence, as if all the lungs of the earth had ceased breathing so as not to break the soft silence of the air. He felt as happy as a child face up on the thick, cool grass contemplating a high cloud flying off in the afternoon sky. He was happy, even though he knew he was dead, that he would rest forever in the box lined with artificial silk. He had great lucidity. It was not as before, after his first death, in which he felt dull, listless. The four candles they had placed around him, which were replaced every three months, had begun to go out again, just when they would be indispensable. He felt the closeness of the fresh, damp violets his mother had brought that morning. He felt it in the lilies, the roses. But all that terrible reality did not give him any anxiety. Quite the opposite, he was happy there, alone in his solitude. Would he feel fear afterward?

Who can say? It was hard to think about the moment when the hammer would pound the nails into the green wood and the coffin would creak under its certain hope of becoming a tree once more. His body, drawn now with greater force by the imperative of the earth, would remain tilted in a damp, claylike, soft depth and up there, four cubic yards above, the gravediggers' last blows would grow faint. No. He wouldn't feel fear there either. That would be the prolongation of his death, the most natural prolongation of his new state.

Not even a degree of heat would be left in his body, his medulla would have frozen forever and little ice stars would penetrate as deep as the marrow of his bones. How well he would grow used to his new life as a dead man! One day, however, he will feel his solid armor fall apart, and when he tries to name, review, each one of his members, he won't find them. He will feel that he doesn't have any definitive, exact form, and he will know with resignation that he has lost his perfect twenty-five-year-old anatomy and has been changed into a handful of shapeless dust, with no geometric definition.

The biblical dust of death. Perhaps then he will feel a slight nostalgia, the nostalgia of not being a formal, anatomical corpse, but, rather, an imaginary, abstract corpse, assembled only in the hazy memory of his kin. He will know then that he will rise up the capillary vessels of an apple tree and awaken, bitten by the hunger of a child on some autumn day. He will know—and that did sadden him—that he has lost his unity: that he is no longer even an ordinary dead man, a common corpse.

He had spent that last night in the solitary company of his own corpse.

But with the new day, with the penetration of the first rays of the lukewarm sun through the open window, he felt his skin softening. He observed it for a moment. Quiet, rigid. He let the air run over his body. There was no doubt about it: the "smell" was there. During the night the corpse rot had begun to have its effects. His organism had begun to decompose, rot, like the bodies of all dead people. The "smell" was undoubtedly, unmistakably, the smell of gamy meat, disappearing and then reappearing, more penetrating. His body was decomposing with the heat of the previous night. Yes. He was rotting. Within a few hours his mother would come to change the flowers and the stench of decomposed flesh would hit her from the threshold. Then they would take him away to sleep his second death among the other dead.

But suddenly fear struck him in the back like a dagger.

Fear! Such a deep word, so meaningful! Now he really was afraid, with a true, "physical" fear. What was its cause? He understood perfectly and it made his flesh creep: he probably wasn't dead. They'd put him there, in that box, which now seemed so perfectly soft, so cushioned, so terribly comfortable, and the phantom of fear opened the window of reality to him: They were going to bury him alive!

He couldn't be dead because he had an exact awareness of everything: of the life that was spinning and murmuring about him. Of the warm smell of heliotrope that came in through the open window and mingled with the other "smell." He was quite aware of the slow dripping of the water in the cistern. Of the cricket that had stayed in the corner and was still chirping, thinking that early morning was still there.

Everything denied his death. Everything except the "smell." But how could he know that the smell was his? Maybe his mother had forgotten to change the water in the vases the day before and the stems were rotting. Or maybe the mouse which the cat had dragged into his room had decomposed with the heat. No. The "smell" couldn't be coming from his body.

A few moments before he had been happy with his death, because he had thought he was dead. Because a dead man can be happy with his irremediable situation. But a living person can't resign himself to being buried alive. Yet his members wouldn't respond to his call. He couldn't express himself and that was what caused his terror, the greatest terror of his life and of his death. They were going to bury him alive. He might be able to feel, be aware of the moment they nailed up the box. He would feel the emptiness of the body suspended across the shoulders of friends as his anguish and desperation grew with every step of the procession.

He will try to rise up in vain, to call with all his weakened forces, to pound inside the dark and narrow coffin so that they will know that he is still alive, that they are going to bury him alive. It would be useless. Even there his members would not respond to that urgent and last call of his nervous system.

He heard sounds in the next room. Could he have been asleep? Could all that life of a dead man have been a nightmare? But the sound of the dishes didn't go on. He became sad and maybe he was annoyed because of it. He would have wanted all the dishes in the world to break in one single crash right there beside him, to be awakened by an outside cause since his own will had failed.

But no. It wasn't a dream. He was sure that if it had been a dream his last intent to return to reality wouldn't have failed. He wouldn't wake up again. He felt the softness of the coffin, and the "smell" had returned with greater strength now, with so much strength that he already doubted that it was his own smell. He would have liked to see his relatives there before he began to fall apart, and the spectacle of putrefying flesh would have produced a revulsion in them. The neighbors would flee in fright from the casket, holding a handkerchief to their mouths. They would spit. No. Not that. It would be better if they buried him. It would be better to get out of "that" as soon as possible. Even he now wanted to be quit of his own corpse. Now he knew that he was truly dead, or, at least, inappreciably alive. What difference did it make? The "smell" persisted in any case.

He would hear the last prayers with resignation, the last

Latin mouthings and the acolytes' incompetent response. The cold of the cemetery, filled with dust and bones, would penetrate down even to his bones and dissipate the "smell" a bit, perhaps. Perhaps—who knows!—the imminence of the moment will bring him out of that lethargy. When he feels himself swimming in his own sweat, in a viscous, thick water, as he had swum in the uterus of his mother before being born. Perhaps he is alive, then.

But most likely he is so resigned to dying now that he might well die of resignation.

1947

The Other Side of Death

WITHOUT KNOWING WHY, he awoke with a start. A
sharp smell of violets and formaldehyde, robust and broad,
was coming from the other room, mingling with the aroma
of the newly opened flowers sent out by the dawning garden. He tried to calm down, to recover the spirit he had
suddenly lost in sleep. It must have been dawn now, because outside, in the garden, the sprinkler had begun to
sing amidst the vegetables and the sky was blue through the
open window. He looked about the shadowy room, trying
to explain that sudden, unexpected awakening. He had the
impression, the *physical* certainty, that someone had come
in while he had been asleep. Yet he was alone, and the
door, locked from the inside, showed no signs of violence.
Up above the air over the window a morning star was awak-

ening. He was quiet for a moment, as if trying to loosen the
nervous tension that had pushed him to the surface of
sleep, and closing his eyes, face up, he began to seek the
broken thread of serenity again. His clustered blood broke
up in his throat and beyond that, in his chest, his heart
despaired robustly, marking, marking an accentuated and
light rhythm as if it were coming from some headlong running. He reviewed the previous minutes in his mind. Maybe
he'd had a strange dream. It might have been a nightmare.
No. There was nothing particular, no reason for any start
in "that."

They were traveling in a train—I remember it now—
through a countryside—I've had this dream frequently—
like a still life, sown with false, artificial trees bearing fruit
of razors, scissors, and other diverse items—I remember
now that I have to get my hair cut—barbershop instruments. He'd had that dream a lot of times but it had never
produced that scare in him. There behind a tree was his
brother, the other one, his twin, signaling—this happened
to me somewhere in real life—for him to stop the train.
Convinced of the futility of his message, he began to run
after the coach until he fell, panting, his mouth full of froth.
It was his absurd, irrational dream, of course, but there was
no reason for it to have caused that restless awakening. He
closed his eyes again, his temples still pounded by the current of blood that was rising firmly in him like a clenched
fist. The train went into an arid, sterile, boring geography,
and a pain he felt in his left leg made him turn his attention
from the landscape. He observed that on his middle toe—
I mustn't keep on wearing these tight shoes—he had a
tumor. In a natural way, and as if he were used to it, he took
a screwdriver out of his pocket and extracted the head of

the tumor with it. He placed it carefully in a little blue box —can you see colors in dreams?—and he glimpsed, peeping out of the wound, the end of a greasy, yellow string. Without getting upset, as if he had expected that string to be there, he pulled on it slowly with careful precision. It was a long, a very long tape, which came out by itself, with no discomfort or pain. A second later he lifted his eyes and saw that the railway coach had emptied out and that the only one left, in another compartment of the train, was his brother, dressed as a woman, in front of a mirror, trying to extract his left eye with a pair of scissors.

Actually, he was displeased with that dream, but he couldn't explain why it had altered his circulation, because on previous occasions when his nightmares had been hair-raising he had managed to maintain his calm. His hands felt cold. The smell of violets and formaldehyde persisted and became disagreeable, almost aggressive. With his eyes closed, trying to break the rising tempo of his breathing, he tried to find some trivial theme so he could sink into the dream that had been interrupted minutes before. He could think, for example, that in three hours I must go to the funeral parlor to cover the expenses. In the corner a wakeful cricket had raised its chirp and was filling the room with its sharp and cutting throat. The nervous tension began to recede slowly but effectively and he noticed once more the looseness, the laxity of his muscles. He felt that he had fallen on the soft and thick cushion while his body, light and weightless, had been run through by a sweet feeling of beatitude and fatigue and was losing consciousness of its own material structure, that heavy, earthy substance that defined it, placing it in an unmistakable and exact spot on the zoological scale and bearing a whole sum of systems, geometrically defined organs that lifted him up to the arbitrary hierarchy of rational animals. His eyelids, docile now, fell over his corneas in the same natural way with which his arms and legs mingled in a gathering of members that were slowly losing their independence, as if the whole organism had turned into one single, large, total organism, and he—the man—had abandoned his mortal roots so as to penetrate other, deeper and firmer, roots: the eternal roots of an integral and definitive dream. Outside, from the other side of the world, he could hear the cricket's song growing weaker until it disappeared from his senses, which had turned inward, submerging him in a new and uncomplicated notion of time and space, erasing the presence of that material world, physical and painful, full of insects and acrid smells of violets and formaldehyde.

Gently wrapped in the warm climate of a coveted serenity, he felt the lightness of his artificial and daily death. He sank into a loving geography, into an easy, ideal world, a world like one drawn by a child, with no algebraic equations, with no loving farewells, no force of gravity.

He wasn't exactly sure how long he'd been like that, between that noble surface of dreams and realities, but he did remember that suddenly, as if his throat had been cut by the slash of a knife, he'd given a start in bed and felt that his twin brother, his dead brother, was sitting on the edge of the bed.

Again, as before, his heart was a fist that rose up into his mouth and pushed him into a leap. The dawning light, the cricket that continued grinding the solitude with its little out-of-tune hand organ, the cool air that came up from the garden's universe, everything contributed to make him return to the real world once more. But this time he could understand what had caused his start. During the brief minutes of his dozing, and—I can see it now—during the whole night, when he had thought he'd had a peaceful, simple sleep, *with no thoughts,* his memory had been fixed on one single, constant, invariable image, an *autonomous* image that imposed itself on his thought in spite of the will and the resistance of the thought itself. Yes. Almost without his noticing it, "that" thought had been overpowering him, filling him, completely inhabiting him, turning into a backdrop that was fixed there behind the other thoughts, giving support, the definitive vertebrae to the mental drama of his day and night. The idea of his twin brother's corpse had been firmly stuck in the whole center of his life. And now that they had left him there, in his parcel of land now, his eyelids fluttered by the rain, now *he was afraid* of him.

He never thought the blow would have been so strong. Through the partly opened window the smell entered again, mixed in now with a different smell, of damp earth, submerged bones, and his sense of smell came out to meet it joyfully, with the tremendous happiness of a bestial man. Many hours had already passed since the moment in which *he saw* it twisting like a badly wounded dog under the sheets, howling, biting out that last shout that filled his throat with salt, using his nails to try to break the pain that was climbing up *him,* along his back, to the roots of the tumor. He couldn't forget *his* thrashing like a dying animal, rebellious at the truth that had stopped in front of *him,* that had clasped *his* body with tenacity, with imperturbable constancy, something definitive, like death itself. He saw *him* during the last moments of *his* barbarous death throes. When he broke *his* nails against the walls, clawing at that last piece of life which was slipping away through his fingers, bleeding *him*, while the gangrene *was getting into him* through the side like an implacable woman. Then he saw *him* fall onto the messy bed, with a touch of resigned fatigue, sweating, as his froth-covered teeth drew a horrible, monstrous smile for the world out of him and death began to flow through his bones like a river of ashes.

It was then that I thought about the tumor that had ceased to pain in his stomach. I imagined it as round—now he felt the same sensation—swelling like an interior sun, unbearable like a yellow insect extending its vicious filaments toward the depths of the intestines. (He felt that his viscera had become dislocated inside him as before the imminence of a physiological necessity.) Maybe I'll have a tumor like his someday. At first it will be a small but growing sphere that will branch out, growing larger in my stomach like a fetus. I will probably feel it when it starts to take on motion, moving inward with the fury of a sleepwalking child, traveling through my intestines blindly—he put his hands on his stomach to contain the sharp pain—its anxious hands held out toward the shadows, looking for the warm matrix, the hospitable uterus that it is never to find; while its hundred feet of a fantastic animal will go on wrapping themselves up into a long and yellow umbilical cord. Yes. Maybe I—the stomach—like this brother who has just died, have a tumor at the root of my viscera. The smell that the garden had sent was returning now, strong, repugnant, enveloped in a nauseating stench. Time seemed to have stopped on the edge of dawn. The morning star had jelled on the glass while the neighboring room, where the corpse had been all the night before, was still exuding its strong formaldehyde message. It was, certainly, a different smell from that of the garden. This was a more anguished, a more specific smell than that mingled smell of unequal flowers. A smell that always, once it was known, was related to corpses. It was the glacial and exuberant smell left with him from the formic aldehyde of amphitheaters. He thought about the laboratory. He remembered the viscera preserved in absolute alcohol; the dissected birds. A rabbit saturated with formaldehyde has its flesh harden, it becomes dehydrated and loses its docile elasticity until it changes into a perpetual, eternalized rabbit. Formaldehyde. Where is this smell coming from? *The only way to contain rot.* If we men *had* formaldehyde in our veins *we would be* like the anatomical specimens submerged in absolute alcohol.

There outside he heard the beating of the increasing rain as it came hammering on the glass of the partly open window. A cool, joyful, and new air came in, loaded with dampness. The cold of his hands intensified, making him feel the presence of the formaldehyde in his arteries; as if the dampness of the courtyard had come into him down to the bones. Dampness. There's a lot of dampness "there." With a certain displeasure he thought about the winter nights when the rain will pass through the grass and the dampness will come to rest on his brother's side, circulate through his body like a concrete current. It seemed to him that the dead had need of a different circulatory system that hurled them toward another irremediable and final death. At that moment he didn't want it to rain any more, he wanted summer to be an eternal, dominant season. Because of his thoughts, he was displeased by the persistence of that damp clatter on the glass. He wanted the clay of cemeteries to be dry, always dry, because it made him restless to think that after two weeks, when the dampness begins to run through the marrow, there would no longer be another man equal, exactly equal to him under the ground.

Yes. *They* were twin brothers, exact, whom no one could distinguish at first sight. Before, when they both were living their separate lives, they were nothing but *two twin brothers,* simple and apart like two different men. *Spiritually* there was no common factor between them. But now, when rigidity, the terrible reality, was climbing up along his back like an invertebrate animal, something had dissolved in his integral atmosphere, something that sounded like an emptiness, as if a precipice had opened up at his side, or as if his body had suddenly been sliced in two by an ax; not that exact, anatomical body under a perfect geometrical definition; not that physical body that now felt fear; another body, rather, that was coming from beyond his, that had been sunken with him in the liquid night of the maternal womb and was climbing up with him through the branches of an ancient genealogy; that was with him in the blood of his four pairs of great-grandparents and that came from way back, from the beginning of the world, sustaining with its weight, with its mysterious presence, the whole universal balance. It might be that he had been in the blood of Isaac and Rebecca, that it was his other brother who had been born shackled to his heel and who came tumbling along generation after generation, night after night, from kiss to kiss, from love to love, descending through arteries and testicles until he arrived, as on a night voyage at the womb of his recent mother. The mysterious ancestral itinerary was being presented to him now as painful and true, now that the equilibrium had been broken and the equation definitively solved. He knew that something was lacking for his personal harmony, his formal and everyday integrity:

Jacob had been irremediably freed from his ankles!

During the days when his brother was ill he hadn't had this feeling, because the emaciated face, transfigured by fever and pain, with the grown beard, had been quite different from his.

Once he was motionless, lying out on top of his total death, a barber was called to "arrange" the corpse. He was present, leaning tightly against the wall, when the man dressed in white arrived bearing the clean instruments of his profession. . . . With the precision of a master he covered the dead man's beard with lather—the frothy mouth: that was how I saw him before he died—and slowly, as one who goes about revealing a tremendous secret, he began to shave him. It was then that he was assaulted by "that" terrible idea. As the pale and earthen face of his twin brother emerged under the passage of the razor, he had the feeling that the corpse there was not *a thing* that was alien to him but was made from his same earthy substance, that it was his own repetition. . . . He had the strange feeling that his kin had extracted his image from the mirror, the one he saw reflected in the glass when he shaved. Now that image, which used to respond to every movement of his, had gained independence. He had watched it being shaved other times, every morning. But now he was witnessing the dramatic experience of another man's taking the beard off the image in his mirror, his own physical presence unneeded. He had the certainty, the assurance, that if he had gone over to a mirror at that moment he would have found it blank, even though physics had no precise explanation for the phenomenon. It was an awareness of splitting in two! His double was a corpse! Desperate, trying to react, he touched the firm wall that rose up in him by touch, a kind of current of security. The barber finished his work and with the tip of his scissors closed the corpse's eyelids. Night left him trembling inside, with the irrevocable solitude of the plucked corpse. That was how exact they were. Two identical brothers, disquietingly repeated.

It was then, as he observed how intimately joined those two natures were, that it occurred to him that something extraordinary, something unexpected, was going to happen. He imagined that the separation of the two bodies in space was just appearance, while in reality the two of them had a single, total nature. Maybe when organic decomposition reaches the dead one, he, the living one, will begin to decay also within his animated world.

He could hear the rain beating more strongly on the panes and the cricket suddenly snapped his string. His hands were now intensely cold with a long, dehumanized coldness. The smell of formaldehyde, stronger now, made him think about the possibility of reaching the rottenness that his twin brother was communicating to him from there, from his frozen hole in the ground. That's absurd! Maybe the phenomenon is the opposite: the influence must be exercised by the one who remained with life, with his energy, with his vital cell! Maybe—on this level—he and his brother, too, will remain intact, sustaining a balance between life and death as they defend themselves against putrefaction. But who can be sure of it? Wasn't it just as possible that the buried brother would remain incorruptible while rottenness would invade the living one with all its blue octopuses?

He thought that the last hypothesis was the most probable and resigned himself to wait for the arrival of his tremendous hour. His flesh had become soft, adipose, and he thought he could feel a blue substance covering him all over. He sniffed down below for the coming of his own bodily odors, but only the formaldehyde from the next room agitated his olfactory membranes with an icy, unmistakable shudder. Nothing worried him after that. The cricket in its corner tried to start its ballad up again while a thick, exact drop began to run along the ceiling in the very center of the room. He heard it drop without surprise because he knew that the wood was old in that spot, but he imagined that drop, formed from cool, good, friendly water, coming from the sky, from a better life, one that was broader and not so full of idiotic phenomena like love or digestion or twinship. Maybe that drop would fill the room in the space of an hour or in a thousand years and would dissolve that mortal armor, that vain substance, which perhaps—why not?—between brief instants would be nothing but a sticky mixture of albumen and whey. Everything was equal now. Only his own death came between him and his grave. Resigned, he listened to the drop, thick, heavy, exact, as it dripped in the other world, in the mistaken and absurd world of rational creatures.

(1948)

Eva Is Inside Her Cat

ALL OF A SUDDEN SHE NOTICED that her beauty had
fallen all apart on her, that it had begun to pain her physi-
cally like a tumor or a cancer. She still remembered the
weight of the privilege she had borne over her body during
adolescence, which she had dropped now—who knows
where?—with the weariness of resignation, with the final
gesture of a declining creature. It was impossible to bear
that burden any longer. She had to drop that useless attri-
bute of her personality somewhere; as she turned a corner,
somewhere in the outskirts. Or leave it behind on the coat-
rack of a second-rate restaurant like some old useless coat.
She was tired of being the center of attention, of being
under siege from men's long looks. At night, when insomnia stuck its pins into her eyes, she would have liked to be

an ordinary woman, without any special attraction. Everything was hostile to her within the four walls of her room. Desperate, she could feel her vigil spreading out under her skin, into her head, pushing the fever upward toward the roots of her hair. It was as if her arteries had become peopled with hot, tiny insects who, with the approach of dawn, awoke each day and ran about on their moving feet in a rending subcutaneous adventure in that place of clay made fruit where her anatomical beauty had found its home. In vain she struggled to chase those terrible creatures away. She couldn't. They were part of her own organism. They'd been there, alive, since much before her physical existence. They came from the heart of her father, who had fed them painfully during his nights of desperate solitude. Or maybe they had poured into her arteries through the cord that linked her to her mother ever since the beginning of the world. There was no doubt that those insects had not been born spontaneously inside her body. She knew that they came from back there, that all who bore her surname had to bear them, had to suffer them as she did when insomnia held unconquerable sway until dawn. It was those very insects who painted that bitter expression, that unconsolable sadness on the faces of her forebears. She had seen them looking out of their extinguished existence, out of their ancient portraits, victims of that same anguish. She still remembered the disquieting face of the great-grandmother who, from her aged canvas, begged for a minute of rest, a second of peace from those insects who there, in the channels of her blood, kept on martyrizing her, pitilessly beautifying her. No. Those insects didn't belong to her. They came, transmitted from generation to generation, sustaining with their tiny armor all the prestige of a select caste, a painfully select group. Those insects had been born in the womb of the first woman who had had a beautiful daughter. But it was necessary, urgent, to put a stop to that heritage. Someone must renounce the eternal transmission of that artificial beauty. It was no good for women of her breed to admire themselves as they came back from their mirrors if during the night those creatures did their slow, effective, ceaseless work with a constancy of centuries. It was no longer beauty, it was a sickness that had to be halted, that had to be cut off in some bold and radical way.

She still remembered the endless hours spent on that bed sown with hot needles. Those nights when she tried to speed time along so that with the arrival of daylight the beasts would stop hurting her. What good was beauty like that? Night after night, sunken in her desperation, she thought it would have been better for her to have been an ordinary woman, or a man. But that useless virtue was denied her, fed by insects of remote origin who were has-tening the irrevocable arrival of her death. Maybe she would have been happy if she had had the same lack of grace, that same desolate ugliness, as her Czechoslovakian friend who had a dog's name. She would have been better off ugly, so that she could sleep peacefully like any other Christian.

She cursed her ancestors. They were to blame for her insomnia. They had transmitted that exact, invariable beauty, as if after death mothers shook and renewed their heads in order to graft them onto the trunks of their daugh-ters. It was as if the same head, a single head, had been continuously transmitted, with the same ears, the same nose, the identical mouth, with its weighty intelligence, to all the women who were to receive it irremediably like a painful inheritance of beauty. It was there, in the transmission of the head, that the eternal microbe that came through across generations had been accentuated, had taken on personality, strength, until it became an invincible being, an incurable illness, which upon reaching her after having passed through a complicated process of judgment, could no longer be borne and was bitter and painful . . . just like a tumor or a cancer.

It was during those hours of wakefulness that she remembered the things disagreeable to her fine sensibility. She remembered the objects that made up the sentimental universe where, as in a chemical stew, those microbes of despair had been cultivated. During those nights, with her big round eyes open and frightened, she bore the weight of the darkness that fell upon her temples like molten lead. Everything was asleep around her. And from her corner, in order to bring on sleep, she tried to go back over her childhood memories.

But that remembering always ended with a terror of the unknown. Always, after wandering through the dark corners of the house, her thoughts would find themselves face to face with fear. Then the struggle would begin. The real struggle against three unmovable enemies. She would never—no, she would never—be able to shake the fear from her head. She would have to bear it as it clutched at her throat. And all just to live in that ancient mansion, to sleep alone in that corner, away from the rest of the world.

Her thoughts always went down along the damp, dark passageways, shaking the dry cobweb-covered dust off the portraits. That disturbing and fearsome dust that fell from above, from the place where the bones of her ancestors were falling apart. Invariably she remembered the "boy."

She imagined him there, sleepwalking under the grass in the courtyard beside the orange tree, a handful of wet earth in his mouth. She seemed to see him in his clay depths, digging upward with his nails, his teeth, fleeing the cold that bit into his back, looking for the exit into the courtyard through that small tunnel where they had placed him along with the snails. In winter she would hear him weeping with his tiny sob, mud-covered, drenched with rain. She imagined him intact. Just as they had left him five years before in that water-filled hole. She couldn't think of him as having decomposed. On the contrary, he was probably most handsome sailing along in that thick water as on a voyage with no escape. Or she saw him alive but frightened, afraid of feeling himself alone, buried in such a somber courtyard. She herself had been against their leaving him there, under the orange tree, so close to the house. She was afraid of him. She knew that on nights when insomnia hounded her he would sense it. He would come back along the wide corridors to ask her to stay with him, ask her to defend him against those other insects, who were eating at the roots of his violets. He would come back to have her let him sleep beside her as he did when he was alive. She was afraid of feeling him beside her again after he had leaped over the wall of death. She was afraid of stealing those hands that the "boy" would always keep closed to warm up his little piece of ice. She wished, after she saw him turned into cement, like the statue of fear fallen in the mud, she wished that they would take him far away so that she wouldn't remember him at night. And yet they had left him there, where he was imperturbable now, wretched, feeding his blood with the mud of earthworms. And she had to resign herself to seeing him return from the depths of his shad-

ows. Because always, invariably, when she lay awake she
began to think about the "boy," who must be calling her
from his piece of earth to help him flee that absurd death.

But now, in her new life, temporal and spaceless, she was
more tranquil. She knew that outside her world there, everything would keep going on with the same rhythm as
before; that her room would still be sunken in early-morn-
ing darkness, and her things, her furniture, her thirteen
favorite books, all in place. And that on her unoccupied
bed, the body aroma that filled the void of what had been
a whole woman was only now beginning to evaporate. But
how could "that" happen? How could she, after being a
beautiful woman, her blood peopled by insects, pursued by
the fear of the total night, have the immense, wakeful nightmare now of entering a strange, unknown world where all
dimensions had been eliminated? She remembered. That
night—the night of her passage—had been colder than
usual and she was alone in the house, martyrized by insomnia. No one disturbed the silence, and the smell that came
from the garden was a smell of fear. Sweat broke out on her
body as if the blood in her arteries were pouring out its
cargo of insects. She wanted someone to pass by on the
street, someone who would shout, would shatter that
halted atmosphere. For something to move in nature, for
the earth to move around the sun again. But it was useless.
There was no waking up even for those imbecilic men who
had fallen asleep under her ear, inside the pillow. She, too,
was motionless. The walls gave off a strong smell of fresh
paint, that thick, grand smell that you don't smell with your
nose but with your stomach. And on the table the single
clock, pounding on the silence with its mortal machinery.
"Time . . . oh, time!" she sighed, remembering death. And

there in the courtyard, under the orange tree, the "boy" was still weeping with his tiny sob from the other world.

She took refuge in all her beliefs. Why didn't it dawn right then and there or why didn't she die once and for all? She had never thought that beauty would cost her so many sacrifices. At that moment—as usual—it still pained her on top of her fear. And underneath her fear those implacable insects were still martyrizing her. Death had squeezed her into life like a spider, biting her in a rage, ready to make her succumb. But the final moment was taking its time. Her hands, those hands that men squeezed like imbeciles with manifest animal nervousness, were motionless, paralyzed by fear, by that irrational terror that came from within, with no motive, just from knowing that she was abandoned in that ancient house. She tried to react and couldn't. Fear had absorbed her completely and remained there, fixed, tenacious, almost corporeal, as if it were some invisible person who had made up his mind not to leave her room. And the most upsetting part was that the fear had no justification at all, that it was a unique fear, without any reason, a fear just because.

The saliva had grown thick on her tongue. That hard gum that stuck to her palate and flowed because she was unable to contain it was bothersome between her teeth. It was a desire that was quite different from thirst. A superior desire that she was feeling for the first time in her life. For a moment she forgot about her beauty, her insomnia, and her irrational fear. She didn't recognize herself. For an instant she thought that the microbes had left her body. She felt that they'd come out stuck to her saliva. Yes, that was all very fine. It was fine that the insects no longer occupied her and that she could sleep now, but she had to find a way to dissolve that resin that dulled her tongue. If she could only get to the pantry and . . . But what was she thinking about? She gave a start of surprise. She'd never felt "that desire." The urgency of the acidity had debilitated her, rendering useless the discipline that she had faithfully followed for so many years ever since the day they had buried the "boy." It was foolish, but she felt revulsion about eating an orange. She knew that the "boy" had climbed up to the orange blossoms and that the fruit of next autumn would be swollen with his flesh, cooled by the coolness of his death. No. She couldn't eat them. She knew that under every orange tree in the world there was a boy buried, sweetening the fruit with the lime of his bones. Nevertheless, she had to eat an orange now. It was the only thing for that gum that was smothering her. It was foolishness to think that the "boy" was inside a fruit. She would take advantage of that moment in which beauty had stopped paining her to get to the pantry. But wasn't that strange? It was the first time in her life that she'd felt a real urge to eat an orange. She became happy, happy. Oh, what pleasure! Eating an orange. She didn't know why, but she'd never had such a demanding desire. She would get up, happy to be a normal woman again, singing merrily until she got to the pantry, singing merrily like a new woman, newborn. She would even get to the courtyard and . . .

Her memory was suddenly cut off. She remembered that she had tried to get up and that she was no longer in her bed, that her body had disappeared, that her thirteen favorite books were no longer there, that she was no longer she, now that she was bodiless, floating, drifting over an absolute nothingness, changed into an amorphous dot, tiny, lacking direction. She was unable to pinpoint what had happened. She was confused. She just had the sensation that someone had pushed her into space from the top of a precipice. She felt changed into an abstract, imaginary being. She felt changed into an incorporeal woman, something like her suddenly having entered that high and unknown world of pure spirits.

She was afraid again. But it was a different fear from what she had felt a moment before. It was no longer the fear of the "boy" 's weeping. It was a terror of the strange, of what was mysterious and unknown in her new world. And to think that all of it had happened so innocently, with so much naïveté on her part. What would she tell her mother when she told her what had happened when she got home? She began to think about how alarmed the neighbors would be when they opened the door to her bedroom and discovered that the bed was empty, that the locks had not been touched, that no one had been able to enter or to leave, and that, none the less, she wasn't there. She imagined her mother's desperate movements as she searched through the room, conjecturing, wondering "what could have become of that girl?" The scene was clear to her. The neighbors would arrive and begin to weave comments together —some of them malicious—concerning her disappearance. Each would think according to his own and particular way of thinking. Each would try to offer the most logical explanation, the most acceptable, at least, while her mother would run along all the corridors in the big house, desperate, calling her by name.

And there she would be. She would contemplate the moment, detail by detail, from a corner, from the ceiling, from the chinks in the wall, from anywhere; from the best angle, shielded by her bodiless state, in her spacelessness.

It bothered her, thinking about it. Now she realized her mistake. She wouldn't be able to give any explanation, clear anything up, console anybody. No living being could be informed of her transformation. Now—perhaps the only time that she needed them—she wouldn't have a mouth, arms, so that everybody could know that she was there, in her corner, separated from the three-dimensional world by an unbridgeable distance. In her new life she was isolated, completely prevented from grasping emotions. But at every moment something was vibrating in her, a shudder that ran through her, overwhelming her, making her aware of that other physical universe that moved outside her world. She couldn't hear, she couldn't see, but she *knew* about that sound and that sight. And there, in the heights of her superior world, she began to know that an environment of anguish surrounded her.

Just a moment before—according to our temporal world —she had made the passage, so that only now was she beginning to know the peculiarities, the characteristics, of her new world. Around her an absolute, radical darkness spun. How long would that darkness last? Would she have to get used to it for eternity? Her anguish grew from her concentration as she saw herself sunken in that thick impenetrable fog: could she be in limbo? She shuddered. She remembered everything she had heard about limbo. If she really was there, floating beside her were other pure spirits, those of children who had died without baptism, who had been dying for a thousand years. In the darkness she tried to find next to her those beings who must have been much purer, ever so much simpler, than she. Completely isolated from the physical world, condemned to a sleepwalking and eternal life. Maybe the "boy" was there looking for an exit that would lead him to his body.

But no. Why should she be in limbo? Had she died, perhaps? No. It was simply a change in state, a normal passage from the physical world to an easier, uncomplicated world, where all dimensions had been eliminated.

Now she would not have to bear those subterranean insects. Her beauty had collapsed on her. Now, in that elemental situation, she could be happy. Although—oh!—not completely happy, because now her greatest desire, the desire to eat an orange, had become impossible. It was the only thing that might have caused her still to want to be in her first life. To be able to satisfy the urgency of the acidity that still persisted after the passage. She tried to orient herself so as to reach the pantry and feel, if nothing else, the cool and sour company of the oranges. It was then that she discovered a new characteristic of her world: she was everywhere in the house, in the courtyard, on the roof, even in the "boy" 's orange tree. She was in the whole physical world there beyond. And yet she was nowhere. She became upset again. She had lost control over herself. Now she was under a superior will, she was a useless being, absurd, good for nothing. Without knowing why, she began to feel sad. She almost began to feel nostalgia for her beauty: for the beauty that had foolishly ruined her.

But one supreme idea reanimated her. Hadn't she heard, perhaps, that pure spirits can penetrate any body at will? After all, what harm was there in trying? She attempted to remember what inhabitant of the house could be put to the proof. If she could fulfill her aim she would be satisfied: she could eat the orange. She remembered. At that time the servants were usually not there. Her mother still hadn't arrived. But the need to eat an orange, joined now to the curiosity of seeing herself incarnate in a body different from her own, obliged her to act at once. And yet there was no one there in whom she could incarnate herself. It was a desolating bit of reason: there was nobody in the house. She would have to live eternally isolated from the outside world, in her undimensional world, unable to eat the first orange. And all because of a foolish thing. It would have been better to go on bearing up for a few more years under that hostile beauty and not wipe herself out forever, making herself useless, like a conquered beast. But it was too late.

She was going to withdraw, disappointed, into a distant region of the universe, to a place where she could forget all her earthly desires. But something made her suddenly hold back. The promise of a better future had opened up in her unknown region. Yes, there was someone in the house in whom she could reincarnate herself: the cat! Then she hesitated. It was difficult to resign herself to live inside an animal. She would have soft, white fur, and a great energy for a leap would probably be concentrated in her muscles. And she would feel her eyes glow in the dark like two green coals. And she would have white, sharp teeth to smile at her mother from her feline heart with a broad and good animal smile. But no! It couldn't be. She imagined herself quickly inside the body of the cat, running through the corridors of the house once more, managing four uncomfortable legs, and that tail would move on its own, without rhythm, alien to her will. What would life look like through those green and luminous eyes? At night she would go to mew at the sky so that it would not pour its moonlit cement down on the face of the "boy," who would be on his back drinking in the dew. Maybe in her status as a cat she would also feel fear. And maybe, in the end, she would be unable to eat the orange with that carnivorous mouth. A coldness that came from right then and there, born of the very roots of her spirit, quivered in her memory. No. It was impossible to incarnate herself in the cat. She was afraid of one day feeling in her palate, in her throat, in all her quadruped organism, the irrevocable desire to eat a mouse. Probably when her spirit began to inhabit the cat's body she would no longer feel any desire to eat an orange but the repugnant and urgent desire to eat a mouse. She shuddered on thinking about it, caught between her teeth after the chase. She felt it struggling in its last attempts at escape, trying to free itself to get back to its hole again. No. Anything but that. It was preferable to stay there for eternity, in that distant and mysterious world of pure spirits.

But it was difficult to resign herself to live forgotten forever. Why did she have to feel the desire to eat a mouse? Who would rule in that synthesis of woman and cat? Would the primitive animal instinct of the body rule, or the pure will of the woman? The answer was crystal clear. There was no reason to be afraid. She would incarnate herself in the cat and would eat her desired orange. Besides, she would be a strange being, a cat with the intelligence of a beautiful woman. She would be the center of all attention. . . . It was then, for the first time, that she understood that above all her virtues what was in command was the vanity of a metaphysical woman.

Like an insect on the alert which raises its antennae, she put her energy to work throughout the house in search of the cat. It must still be on top of the stove at that time, dreaming that it would wake up with a sprig of heliotrope between its teeth. But it wasn't there. She looked for it again, but she could no longer find the stove. The kitchen wasn't the same. The corners of the house were strange to her; they were no longer those dark corners full of cobwebs. The cat was nowhere to be found. She looked on the roof, in the trees, in the drains, under the bed, in the pantry. She found everything confused. Where she expected to find the portraits of her ancestors again, she found only a bottle of arsenic. From there on she found arsenic all through the house, but the cat had disappeared. The house was no longer the same as before. What had happened to her things? Why were her thirteen favorite books now covered with a thick coat of arsenic? She remembered the orange tree in the courtyard. She looked for it, and tried to find the "boy" again in his pit of water. But the orange tree wasn't in its place and the "boy" was nothing now but a handful of arsenic mixed with ashes underneath a heavy concrete platform. Now she really was going to sleep. Everything was different. And the house had a strong smell of arsenic that beat on her nostrils as if from the depths of a pharmacy.

Only then did she understand that three thousand years had passed since the day she had had a desire to eat the first orange.

(1948)

Dialogue with the Mirror

THE MAN WHO HAD HAD THE ROOM BEFORE, after having slept the sleep of the just for hours on end, oblivious to the worries and unrest of the recent early morning, awoke when the day was well advanced and the sounds of the city completely invaded the air of the half-opened room. He must have thought—since no other state of mind occupied him—about the thick preoccupation of death, about his full, round fear, about the piece of earth—clay of himself—that his brother must have had under his tongue. But the joyful sun that clarified the garden drew his attention toward another life, which was more ordinary, more earthly, and perhaps less true than his fearsome interior existence. Toward his life as an ordinary man, a daily animal, which made him remember—without relying on his nervous system, his changeable liver—the irremediable impossibility of sleeping like a bourgeois. He thought—and there, surely, there was something of bourgeois mathematics in the tongue-twisting figures—of the financial riddles of the office.

Eight-twelve. I will certainly be late. He ran the tips of his fingers over his cheek. The harsh skin, sown with stumps, passed the feeling of the hard hairs through his digital antennae. Then, with the palm of his half-opened hand, he felt his distracted face carefully, with the serene tranquillity of a surgeon who knows the nucleus of the tumor, and from the bland surface toward the inside the hard substance of a truth rose up, one that on occasion had turned him white with anguish. There, under his fingertips—and after the fingertips, bone against bone—his irrevocable anatomical condition held an order of compositions buried, a tight universe of weaves, of lesser worlds, which bore him along, raising his fleshy armor toward a height less enduring than the natural and final position of his bones.

Yes. Against the pillow, his head sunken in the soft material, his body falling into the repose of his organs, life had a horizontal taste, a better accommodation to its own principles. He knew that with the minimum effort of closing his eyes, the long, fatiguing task awaiting him would begin to be resolved in a climate that was becoming uncomplicated, without compromises with either time or space: with no need, when he reached it, for the chemical adventure that made up his body to suffer the slightest impairment. On the contrary, like that, with his eyes closed, there was a total economy of vital resources, an absolute absence of organic wear. His body, sunk in the water of dreams, could move, live, evolve toward other forms of existence where his real world would have, as its intimate necessity, an identical—if not greater—density of motion with which the necessity of living would remain completely satisfied without any detriment to his physical integrity. Much easier—then—would be the chore of living with beings, things, acting, nevertheless, in exactly the same way as in the real world. The chores of shaving, taking the bus, solving equations at the office would be simple and uncomplicated in his dream and would produce in him the same inner satisfaction in the end.

Yes. It was better doing it in that artificial way, as he was already doing; looking in the lighted room for the direction of the mirror. As he would have kept on doing if at that instant a heavy machine, brutal and absurd, had not ruptured the lukewarm substance of his incipient dream. Returning now to the conventional world, the problem certainly took on greater characteristics of seriousness. None the less, the curious theory that had just inspired softness in him had turned him toward a region of understanding, and from within his man-body he felt the displacement of the mouth to the side in an expression which must have been an involuntary smile. "Having to shave when I have to be over the books in twenty minutes. Bath eight minutes, five if I hurry, breakfast seven. Unpleasant old sausages. Mabel's shop: provisions, hardware, drugs, liquors; it's like somebody's box; I've forgotten the name. (The bus breaks down on Tuesdays, seven minutes late.) Pendora. No: Peldora. That's not it. A half hour in all. There's no time. I forgot the name, a word with everything in it. Pedora. It begins with *P*."

With his bathrobe on, in front of the wash basin now, a sleepy face, hair uncombed and no shave, he receives a bored look from the mirror. A quick shudder catches him with a cold thread as he discovers his own dead brother, newly arisen, in that image. The same tired face, the same look that was still not fully awake.

A new movement sent the mirror a quantity of light destined to bring out a pleasant expression, but the simultaneous return of that light brought back to him—going against his plans—a grotesque grimace. Water. The hot flow has opened up torrential, exuberant, and the wave of white, thick steam is interposed between him and the glass. In that way—taking advantage of the interruption with a quick movement—he manages to make an adjustment with his own time and with the time inside the quicksilver.

He rose above the leather strop, filling the mirror with pointed ears, cold metal; and the cloud—breaking up now —shows him the other face again, hazy with physical complications, mathematical laws with which geometry was attempting volume in a new way, a concrete formula for light. There, opposite him, was the face, with a pulse, with throbs of its own presence, transfigured into an expression which was simultaneously a smile and mocking seriousness, appearing in the damp glass which the condensation of vapor had left clean.

He smiled. (It smiled.) He showed—to himself—his tongue. (It showed—to the real one—its tongue.) The one in the mirror had a pasty, yellow tongue: "Your stomach is upset," he diagnosed (a wordless expression) with a grimace. He smiled again. (It smiled again.) But now he could see that there was something stupid, artificial, and false in the smile that was returned to him. He smoothed his hair (it smoothed its hair) with his right hand (left hand), returning the bashful smile at once (and disappearing). He was surprised at his own behavior, standing in front of the mirror and making faces like an idiot. Nevertheless, he thought that everybody behaved the same way in front of a mirror and his indignation was greater then with the certainty that since the world was idiotic, he was only rendering tribute to vulgarity. Eight-seventeen.

He knew that he would have to hurry if he didn't want to be fired from the agency. From that agency that for some time now had been changed into the starting point of his singular daily funeral cortege.

The shaving cream, in contact with the brush, had now raised a bluish whiteness that brought him back from his worries. It was the moment in which the suds came up through his body, through the network of arteries, and facilitated the functioning of his whole vital mechanism. ... Thus, returning to normality, it seemed more comfortable to search his soaped-up brain for the word he wanted to compare Mabel's shop with. Peldora. Mabel's junk shop. Paldora. Provisions or drugs. Or everything at the same time: Pendora.

There were enough suds in the mug. But he kept on rubbing the brush, almost with passion. The childish spectacle of the bubbles gave him the clear joy of a big child as it crept up into his heart, heavy and hard, like cheap liquor. A new effort in search of the syllable would have been sufficient then for the word to burst forth, ripe and brutal; for it to come to the surface in that thick, murky water of his flighty memory. But that time, as on other occasions, the scattered, detached pieces of a single system would not adjust themselves exactly in order to gain organic totality, and he was ready to give up the word forever: Pendora!

And now it was time to desist in that useless search,

because—they both raised their eyes, which met—his twin brother, with his frothy brush, had begun to cover his chin with blue-white coolness, letting his left hand move—he imitated him with the right—with smoothness and precision, until the delineated zone had been covered. He glanced away, and the geometry of the hands on the clock showed itself to him, intent on the solution of a new theorem of anguish: eight-eighteen. He was moving too slowly. So that with the firm aim of finishing quickly, he gripped the razor as the horn handle obeyed the mobility of his little finger.

Calculating that in three minutes the task would be done, he raised his right arm (left arm) to the level of his right ear (left ear), making the observation along the way that nothing should turn out to be as difficult as shaving oneself the way the image in the mirror was doing. From that he had derived a whole series of very complicated calculations with an aim to verifying the speed of the light which, *almost* simultaneously, was making the trip back and forth and reproducing that movement. But the aesthete in him, after a struggle approximately equal to the square root of the velocity he might have found, overcame the mathematician and the artist's thoughts went toward the movements of the blade that greenbluewhited with the various touches of the light. Rapidly—and the mathematician and the aesthete were at peace now—he brought the edge down along the right cheek (left cheek) to the meridian of the lip and observed with satisfaction that the left cheek on the image showed clean between its edges of lather.

He had still not shaken the blade clean when a smokiness loaded with the bitter smell of roasting meat began to arrive from the kitchen. He felt the quiver under his tongue and the torrent of easy, thin saliva that filled his mouth with the energetic taste of hot fat. Fried kidneys. There was finally a change in Mabel's damned store. Pendora. Not that either. The sound of the gland in the midst of the sauce broke in his ear with a memory of hammering rain, which was, in effect, the same from the recent early dawn. Therefore he mustn't forget his galoshes and his raincoat. Kidneys in gravy. No doubt about it.

Of all his senses none deserved as much mistrust as smell. But even beyond his five senses and even when that feast was nothing more than a bit of optimism on the part of his pituitary, the need to finish as soon as possible was at that moment the most urgent need of his five senses. With precision and deftness—the mathematician and the artist showed their teeth—he brought the razor backward (forward) and forward (backward) up to the corner of his mouth to the right (left), while with his left hand (right hand) he smoothed the skin, facilitating in that way the passage of the metal edge, from front (back) to back (front), and up (up) and down, finishing—both panting—the simultaneous work.

But precisely upon finishing, when he was giving the last touches to his left cheek with his right hand, he managed to see his own elbow against the mirror. He saw it, large, strange, unknown, and observed with surprise that above the elbow, other eyes equally large and equally unknown were searching wildly for the direction of the blade. Someone is trying to hang my brother. A powerful arm. Blood! The same thing always happens when I'm in a hurry.

On his face he sought the corresponding place; but his finger was clean and his touch showed no solution of continuity. He gave a start. There were no wounds on his skin, but there in the mirror the other one was bleeding slightly. And inside him the annoyance that last night's upset would be repeated became his truth again, a consciousness of unfolding. But there was the chin (round: identical faces). Those hairs on the mole needed the tip of the razor.

He thought he had observed a cloud of worry haze over the hasty expression of his image. Could it be possible, due to the great rapidity with which he was shaving—and the mathematician took complete charge of the situation—that the velocity of light was unable to cover the distance in order to record all the movements? Could he, in his haste, have got ahead of the image in the mirror and finished the job one motion ahead of it? Or could it have been possible—and the artist, after a brief struggle, managed to dislodge the mathematician— that the image had taken on its own life and had resolved—by living in an uncomplicated time—to finish more slowly than its external subject?

Visibly preoccupied, he turned the hot-water faucet on and felt the rise of the warm, thick steam, while the splashing of his face in the fresh water filled his ears with a guttural sound. On his skin, the pleasant harshness of the freshly laundered towel made him breathe in the deep satisfaction of a hygienic animal. Pandora! That's the word: Pandora.

He looked at the towel with surprise and closed his eyes, disconcerted, while there in the mirror, a face just like his contemplated him with large, stupid eyes and the face was crossed by a crimson thread.

He opened his eyes and smiled (it smiled). Nothing mattered to him any more. Mabel's store is a Pandora's box.

The hot smell of the kidneys in gravy honored his nostrils, with greater urgency now. And he felt satisfaction—positive satisfaction—that a large dog had begun to wag its tail inside his soul.

(1949)

Bitterness for Three Sleepwalkers

Now we had her there, abandoned in a corner of the house. Someone told us, before we brought her things —her clothes which smelled of newly cut wood, her weightless shoes for the mud—that she would be unable to get used to that slow life, with no sweet tastes, no attraction except that harsh, wattled solitude, always pressing on her back. Someone told us—and a lot of time had passed before we remembered it—that she had also had a childhood. Maybe we didn't believe it then. But now, seeing her sitting in the corner with her frightened eyes and a finger placed on her lips, maybe we accepted the fact that she'd had a childhood once, that once she'd had a touch that was sensitive to the anticipatory coolness of the rain, and that she always carried an unexpected shadow in profile to her body.

All this—and much more—we believed that afternoon when we realized that above her fearsome subworld she was completely human. We found it out suddenly, as if a glass had been broken inside, when she began to give off anguished shouts; she began to call each one of us by name, speaking amidst tears until we sat down beside her; we began to sing and clap hands as if our shouting could put the scattered pieces of glass back together. Only then were we able to believe that at one time she had had a childhood. It was as if her shouts were like a revelation somehow; as if they had a lot of remembered tree and deep river about them. When she got up, she leaned over a little and, still without covering her face with her apron, still without blowing her nose, and still with tears, she told us:

"I'll never smile again."

We went out into the courtyard, the three of us, not talking; maybe we thought we carried common thoughts. Maybe we thought it would be best not to turn on the lights in the house. She wanted to be alone—maybe—sitting in the dark corner, weaving the final braid which seemed to be the only thing that would survive her passage toward the beast.

Outside, in the courtyard, sunk in the deep vapor of the insects, we sat down to think about her. We'd done it so many times before. We might have said that we were doing what we'd been doing every day of our lives.

Yet it was different that night: she'd said that she would never smile again, and we, who knew her so well, were certain that the nightmare had become the truth. Sitting in a triangle, we imagined her there inside, abstract, incapacitated, unable even to hear the innumerable clocks that measured the marked and minute rhythm with which she was changing into dust. "If we only had the courage at least to wish for her death," we thought in a chorus. But we wanted her like that: ugly and glacial, like a mean contribution to our hidden defects.

We'd been adults since before, since a long time back. She, however, was the oldest in the house. That same night she had been able to be there, sitting with us, feeling the measured throbbing of the stars, surrounded by healthy sons. She would have been the respectable lady of the house if she had been the wife of a solid citizen or the concubine of a punctual man. But she became accustomed to living in only one dimension, like a straight line, perhaps because her vices or her virtures could not be seen in profile. We'd known that for many years now. We weren't even surprised one morning, after getting up, when we found her face down in the courtyard, biting the earth in a hard, ecstatic way. Then she smiled, looked at us again; she had fallen out of the second-story window onto the hard clay of the courtyard and had remained there, stiff and concrete, face down on the damp clay. But later we learned that the only thing she had kept intact was her fear of distances, a natural fright upon facing space. We lifted her up by the shoulders. She wasn't as hard as she had seemed to us at first. On the contrary, her organs were loose, detached from her will, like a lukewarm corpse that hadn't begun to stiffen.

Her eyes were open, her mouth was dirty with that earth that already must have had a taste of sepulchral sediment for her when we turned her face up to the sun, and it was as if we had placed her in front of a mirror. She looked at us all with a dull, sexless expression that gave us—holding her in my arms now—the measure of her absence. Someone told us she was dead; and afterward she remained smiling with that cold and quiet smile that she wore at night when she moved about the house awake. She said she didn't know how she got to the courtyard. She said that she'd felt quite warm, that she'd been listening to a cricket, penetrating, sharp, which seemed—so she said—about to knock down the wall of her room, and that she had set herself to remembering Sunday's prayers, with her cheek tight against the cement floor.

We knew, however, that she couldn't remember any prayer, for we discovered later that she'd lost the notion of time when she said she'd fallen asleep holding up the inside of the wall that the cricket was pushing on from outside and that she was fast asleep when someone, taking her by the shoulders, moved the wall aside and laid her down with her face to the sun.

That night we knew, sitting in the courtyard, that she would never smile again. Perhaps her inexpressive seriousness pained us in anticipation, her dark and willful living in a corner. It pained us deeply, as we were pained the day we saw her sit down in the corner where she was now; and we heard her say that she wasn't going to wander through the house any more. At first we couldn't believe her. We'd seen her for months on end going through the rooms at all hours, her head hard and her shoulders drooping, never stopping, never growing tired. At night we would hear her thick body noise moving between two darknesses, and we would lie awake in bed many times hearing her stealthy walking, following her all through the house with our ears.

Once she told us that she had seen the cricket inside the mirror glass, sunken, submerged in the solid transparency, and that it had crossed through the glass surface to reach her. We really didn't know what she was trying to tell us, but we could all see that her clothes were wet, sticking to her body, as if she had just come out of a cistern. Without trying to explain the phenomenon, we decided to do away with the insects in the house: destroy the objects that obsessed her.

We had the walls cleaned; we ordered them to chop down the plants in the courtyard and it was as if we had cleansed the silence of the night of bits of trash. But we no longer heard her walking, nor did we hear her talk about crickets any more, until the day when, after the last meal, she remained looking at us, she sat down on the cement floor, still looking at us, and said: "I'm going to stay here, sitting down," and we shuddered, because we could see that she had begun to look like something already almost completely like death.

That had been a long time ago and we had even grown used to seeing her there, sitting, her braid always half wound, as if she had become dissolved in her solitude and, even though she was there to be seen, had lost her natural faculty of being present. That's why we now knew that she would never smile again; because she had said so in the same convinced and certain way in which she had told us once that she would never walk again. It was as if we were certain that she would tell us later: "I'll never see again," or maybe "I'll never hear again," and we knew that she was sufficiently human to go along willing the elimination of her vital functions and that spontaneously she would go about ending herself, sense by sense, until one day we would find her leaning against the wall, as if she had fallen asleep for the first time in her life. Perhaps there was still a lot of time left for that, but the three of us, sitting in the courtyard, would have liked to hear her sharp and sudden broken-glass weeping that night, at least to give us the illusion that a baby . . . a girl baby had been born in the house. In order to believe that she had been born renewed.

(1949)

Eyes of a Blue Dog

THEN SHE LOOKED AT ME. I thought that she was looking at me for the first time. But then, when she turned around behind the lamp and I kept feeling her slippery and oily look in back of me, over my shoulder, I understood that it was I who was looking at her for the first time. I lit a cigarette. I took a drag on the harsh, strong smoke, before spinning in the chair, balancing on one of the rear legs. After that I saw her there, as if she'd been standing beside the lamp looking at me every night. For a few brief minutes that's all we did: look at each other. I looked from the chair, balancing on one of the rear legs. She stood, with a long and quiet hand on the lamp, looking at me. I saw her eyelids lighted up as on every night. It was then that I remembered the usual thing, when I said to her: "Eyes of a blue dog."

Without taking her hand off the lamp she said to me: "That. We'll never forget that." She left the orbit, sighing: "Eyes of a blue dog. I've written it everywhere."

I saw her walk over to the dressing table. I watched her appear in the circular glass of the mirror looking at me now at the end of a back and forth of mathematical light. I watched her keep on looking at me with her great hot-coal eyes: looking at me while she opened the little box covered with pink mother of pearl. I saw her powder her nose. When she finished, she closed the box, stood up again, and walked over to the lamp once more, saying: "I'm afraid that someone is dreaming about this room and revealing my secrets." And over the flame she held the same long and tremulous hand that she had been warming before sitting down at the mirror. And she said: "You don't feel the cold." And I said to her: "Sometimes." And she said to me: "You must feel it now." And then I understood why I couldn't have been alone in the seat. It was the cold that had been giving me the certainty of my solitude. "Now I feel it," I said. "And it's strange because the night is quiet. Maybe the sheet fell off." She didn't answer. Again she began to move toward the mirror and I turned again in the chair, keeping my back to her. Without seeing her, I knew what she was doing. I knew that she was sitting in front of the mirror again, seeing my back, which had had time to reach the depths of the mirror and be caught by her look, which had also had just enough time to reach the depths and return—before the hand had time to start the second turn—until her lips were anointed now with crimson, from the first turn of her hand in front of the mirror. I saw, opposite me, the smooth wall, which was like another blind mirror in which I couldn't see her—sitting behind me—but could imagine her where she probably was as if a mirror had been hung in place of the wall. "I see you," I told her. And on the wall I saw what was as if she had raised her eyes and had seen me with my back turned toward her from the chair, in the depths of the mirror, my face turned toward the wall. Then I saw her lower her eyes again and remain with her eyes always on her brassiere, not talking. And I said to her again: "I see you." And she raised her eyes from her brassiere again. "That's impossible," she said. I asked her why. And she, with her eyes quiet and on her brassiere again: "Because your face is turned toward the wall." Then I spun the chair around. I had the cigarette clenched in my mouth. When I stayed facing the mirror she was back by the lamp. Now she had her hands open over the flame, like the two wings of a hen, toasting herself, and with her face shaded by her own fingers. "I think I'm going to catch cold," she said. "This must be a city of ice." She turned her face to profile and her skin, from copper to red, suddenly became sad. "Do something about it," she said. And she began to get undressed, item by item, starting at the top with the brassiere. I told her: "I'm going to turn back to the wall." She said: "No. In any case, you'll see me the way you did when your back was turned." And no sooner had she said it than she was almost completely undressed, with the flame licking her long copper skin. "I've always wanted to see you like that, with the skin of your belly full of deep pits, as if you'd been beaten." And before I realized that my words had become clumsy at the sight of her nakedness, she became motionless, warming herself on the globe of the lamp, and she said: "Sometimes I think I'm made of metal." She was silent for an instant. The position of her hands over the flame varied slightly. I said: "Sometimes, in other dreams, I've thought you were only a little bronze statue in the corner of some museum. Maybe that's why you're cold." And she said: "Sometimes, when I sleep on my heart, I can feel my body growing hollow and my skin is like plate. Then, when the blood beats inside me, it's as if someone were calling by knocking on my stomach and I can feel my own copper sound in the bed. It's like—what do you call it—laminated metal." She drew closer to the lamp. "I would have liked to hear you," I said. And she said: "If we find each other sometime, put your ear to my ribs when I sleep on the left side and you'll hear me echoing. I've always wanted you to do it sometime." I heard her breathe heavily as she talked. And she said that for years she'd done nothing different. Her life had been dedicated to finding me in reality, through that identifying phrase: "Eyes of a blue dog." And she went along the street saying it aloud, as a way of telling the only person who could have understood her:

"I'm the one who comes into your dreams every night and tells you: 'Eyes of a blue dog.' " And she said that she went into restaurants and before ordering said to the waiters: "Eyes of a blue dog." But the waiters bowed reverently, without remembering ever having said that in their dreams. Then she would write on the napkins and scratch on the varnish of the tables with a knife: "Eyes of a blue dog." And on the steamed-up windows of hotels, stations, all public buildings, she would write with her forefinger: "Eyes of a blue dog." She said that once she went into a drugstore and noticed the same smell that she had smelled in her room one night after having dreamed about me. "He must be near," she thought, seeing the clean, new tiles of the drugstore. Then she went over to the clerk and said to him: "I always dream about a man who says to me: 'Eyes of a blue dog.' " And she said the clerk had looked at her eyes and told her: "As a matter of fact, miss, you do have eyes like that." And she said to him: "I have to find the man who told me those very words in my dreams." And the clerk started to laugh and moved to the other end of the counter. She kept on seeing the clean tile and smelling the odor. And she opened her purse and on the tiles, with her crimson lipstick, she wrote in red letters: "Eyes of a blue dog." The clerk came back from where he had been. He told her: "Madam, you have dirtied the tiles." He gave her a damp cloth, saying: "Clean it up." And she said, still by the lamp, that she had spent the whole afternoon on all fours, washing the tiles and saying: "Eyes of a blue dog," until people gathered at the door and said she was crazy.

Now, when she finished speaking, I remained in the corner, sitting, rocking in the chair. "Every day I try to remember the phrase with which I am to find you," I said. "Now I don't think I'll forget it tomorrow. Still, I've always said the same thing and when I wake up I've always forgotten what the words I can find you with are." And she said: "You invented them yourself on the first day." And I said to her: "I invented them because I saw your eyes of ash. But I never remember the next morning." And she, with clenched fists, beside the lamp, breathed deeply: "If you could at least remember now what city I've been writing it in."

Her tightened teeth gleamed over the flame. "I'd like to touch you now," I said. She raised the face that had been looking at the light; she raised her look, burning, roasting, too, just like her, like her hands, and I felt that she saw me, in the corner where I was sitting, rocking in the chair.

"You'd never told me that," she said. "I tell you now and it's the truth," I said. From the other side of the lamp she asked for a cigarette. The butt had disappeared between my fingers. I'd forgotten that I was smoking. She said: "I don't know why I can't remember where I wrote it." And I said to her: "For the same reason that tomorrow I won't be able to remember the words." And she said sadly: "No. It's just that sometimes I think that I've dreamed that too." I stood up and walked toward the lamp. She was a little beyond, and I kept on walking with the cigarettes and matches in my hand, which would not go beyond the lamp. I held the cigarette out to her. She squeezed it between her lips and leaned over to reach the flame before I had time to light the match. "In some city in the world, on all the walls, those words have to appear in writing: 'Eyes of a blue dog,' " I said. "If I remembered them tomorrow I could find you." She raised her head again and now the lighted coal was between her lips. "Eyes of a blue dog," she sighed, remembered, with the cigarette drooping over her chin and one eye half closed. Then she sucked in the smoke with the cigarette between her fingers and exclaimed: "This is something else now. I'm warming up." And she said it with her voice a little lukewarm and fleeting, as if she hadn't really said it, but as if she had written it on a piece of paper and had brought the paper close to the flame while I read: "I'm warming," and she had continued with the paper between her thumb and forefinger, turning it around as it was being consumed and I had just read ". . . up," before the paper was completely consumed and dropped all wrinkled to the floor, diminished, converted into light ash dust. "That's better," I said. "Sometimes it frightens me to see you that way. Trembling beside a lamp."

We had been seeing each other for several years. Sometimes, when we were already together, somebody would drop a spoon outside and we would wake up. Little by little we'd been coming to understand that our friendship was subordinated to things, to the simplest of happenings. Our meetings always ended that way, with the fall of a spoon early in the morning.

Now, next to the lamp, she was looking at me. I remembered that she had also looked at me in that way in the past, from that remote dream where I made the chair spin on its back legs and remained facing a strange woman with ashen eyes. It was in that dream that I asked her for the first time: "Who are you?" And she said to me: "I don't remember." I said to her: "But I think we've seen each other before." And she said, indifferently: "I think I dreamed about you once, about this same room." And I told her: "That's it. I'm beginning to remember now." And she said: "How strange. It's certain that we've met in other dreams."

She took two drags on the cigarette. I was still standing, facing the lamp, when suddenly I kept looking at her. I looked her up and down and she was still copper; no longer hard and cold metal, but yellow, soft, malleable copper. "I'd like to touch you," I said again. And she said: "You'll ruin everything." I said: "It doesn't matter now. All we have to do is turn the pillow over in order to meet again." And I held my hand out over the lamp. She didn't move. "You'll ruin everything," she said again before I could touch her. "Maybe, if you come around behind the lamp, we'd wake up frightened in who knows what part of the world." But I insisted: "It doesn't matter." And she said: "If we turned over the pillow, we'd meet again. But when you wake up you'll have forgotten." I began to move toward the corner. She stayed behind, warming her hands over the flame. And I still wasn't beside the chair when I heard her say behind me: "When I wake up at midnight, I keep turning in bed, with the fringe of the pillow burning my knee, and repeating until dawn: 'Eyes of a blue dog.' "

Then I remained with my face toward the wall. "It's already dawning," I said without looking at her. "When it struck two I was awake and that was a long time back." I went to the door. When I had the knob in my hand, I heard her voice again, the same, invariable. "Don't open that door," she said. "The hallway is full of difficult dreams." And I asked her: "How do you know?" And she told me: "Because I was there a moment ago and I had to come back when I discovered I was sleeping on my heart." I had the door half opened. I moved it a little and a cold, thin breeze brought me the fresh smell of vegetable earth, damp fields. She spoke again. I gave the turn, still moving the door, mounted on silent hinges, and I told her: "I don't think there's any hallway outside here. I'm getting the smell of country." And she, a little distant, told me: "I know that better than you. What's happening is that there's a woman outside dreaming about the country." She crossed her arms over the flame. She continued speaking: "It's that woman who always wanted to have a house in the country and was never able to leave the city." I remembered having seen the woman in some previous dream, but I knew, with the door ajar now, that within half an hour I would have to go down for breakfast. And I said: "In any case, I have to leave here in order to wake up."

Outside the wind fluttered for an instant, then remained quiet, and the breathing of someone sleeping who had just turned over in bed could be heard. The wind from the fields had ceased. There were no more smells. "Tomorrow I'll recognize you from that," I said. "I'll recognize you when on the street I see a woman writing 'Eyes of a blue dog' on the walls." And she, with a sad smile—which was already a smile of surrender to the impossible, the unreachable—said: "Yet you won't remember anything during the day." And she put her hands back over the lamp, her features darkened by a bitter cloud. "You're the only man who doesn't remember anything of what he's dreamed after he wakes up."

(1950)

The Woman Who Came at Six O'Clock

THE SWINGING DOOR OPENED. At that hour there was nobody in José's restaurant. It had just struck six and the man knew that the regular customers wouldn't begin to arrive until six-thirty. His clientele was so conservative and regular that the clock hadn't finished striking six when a woman entered, as on every day at that hour, and sat down on the stool without saying anything. She had an unlighted cigarette tight between her lips.

"Hello, queen," José said when he saw her sit down. Then he went to the other end of the counter, wiping the streaked surface with a dry rag. Whenever anyone came into the restaurant José did the same thing. Even with the woman, with whom he'd almost come to acquire a degree of intimacy, the fat and ruddy restaurant owner put on his daily comedy of a hard-working man. He spoke from the other end of the counter.

"What do you want today?" he said.

"First of all I want to teach you how to be a gentleman," the woman said. She was sitting at the end of the stools, her elbows on the counter, the extinguished cigarette between her lips. When she spoke, she tightened her mouth so that José would notice the unlighted cigarette.

"I didn't notice," José said.

"You still haven't learned to notice anything," said the woman.

The man left the cloth on the counter, walked to the dark cupboards which smelled of tar and dusty wood, and came back immediately with the matches. The woman leaned over to get the light that was burning in the man's rustic, hairy hands. José saw the woman's lush hair, all greased with cheap, thick Vaseline. He saw her uncovered shoulder above the flowered brassiere. He saw the beginning of her twilight breast when the woman raised her head, the lighted butt between her lips now.

"You're beautiful tonight, queen," José said.

"Stop your nonsense," the woman said. "Don't think that's going to help me pay you."

"That's not what I meant, queen," José said. "I'll bet your lunch didn't agree with you today."

The woman sucked in the first drag of thick smoke, crossed her arms, her elbows still on the counter, and remained looking at the street through the wide restaurant window. She had a melancholy expression. A bored and vulgar melancholy.

"I'll fix you a good steak," José said.

"I still haven't got any money," the woman said.

"You haven't had any money for three months and I always fix you something good," José said.

"Today's different," said the woman somberly, still looking out at the street.

"Every day's the same," José said. "Every day the clock says six, then you come in and say you're hungry as a dog and then I fix you something good. The only difference is this: today you didn't say you were as hungry as a dog but that today is different."

"And it's true," the woman said. She turned to look at the man, who was at the other end of the counter checking the refrigerator. She examined him for two or three seconds. Then she looked at the clock over the cupboard. It was three minutes after six. "It's true, José. Today is different," she said. She let the smoke out and kept on talking with crisp, impassioned words. "I didn't come at six today, that's why it's different, José."

The man looked at the clock.

"I'll cut off my arm if that clock is one minute slow," he said.

"That's not it, José. I didn't come at six o'clock today," the woman said.

"It just struck six, queen," José said. "When you came in it was just finishing."

"I've got a quarter of an hour that says I've been here," the woman said.

José went over to where she was. He put his great puffy face up to the woman while he tugged on one of his eyelids with his index finger.

"Blow on me here," he said.

The woman threw her head back. She was serious, annoyed, softened, beautified by a cloud of sadness and fatigue.

"Stop your foolishness, José. You know I haven't had a drink for six months."

"Tell it to somebody else," he said, "not to me. I'll bet you've had a pint or two at least."

"I had a couple of drinks with a friend," she said.

"Oh, now I understand," José said.

"There's nothing to understand," the woman said. "I've been here for a quarter of an hour."

The man shrugged his shoulders.

"Well, if that's the way you want it, you've got a quarter of an hour that says you've been here," he said. "After all, what difference does it make, ten minutes this way, ten minutes that way?"

"It makes a difference, José," the woman said. And she stretched her arms over the glass counter with an air of careless abandon. She said: "And it isn't that I wanted it that way; it's just that I've been here for a quarter of an hour." She looked at the clock again and corrected herself: "What am I saying—it's been twenty minutes."

"O.K., queen," the man said. "I'd give you a whole day and the night that goes with it just to see you happy."

During all this time José had been moving about behind the counter, changing things, taking something from one place and putting it in another. He was playing his role.

"I want to see you happy," he repeated. He stopped suddenly, turning to where the woman was. "Do you know that I love you very much?"

The woman looked at him coldly.

"Ye-e-es . . .? What a discovery, José. Do you think I'd

go with you even for a million pesos?"

"I didn't mean that, queen," José said. "I repeat, I bet your lunch didn't agree with you."

"That's not why I said it," the woman said. And her voice became less indolent. "No woman could stand a weight like yours, even for a million pesos."

José blushed. He turned his back to the woman and began to dust the bottles on the shelves. He spoke without turning his head.

"You're unbearable today, queen. I think the best thing is for you to eat your steak and go home to bed."

"I'm not hungry," the woman said. She stayed looking out at the street again, watching the passers-by of the dusking city. For an instant there was a murky silence in the restaurant. A peacefulness broken only by José's fiddling about in the cupboard. Suddenly the woman stopped looking out into the street and spoke with a tender, soft, different voice.

"Do you really love me, Pepillo?"

"I do," José said dryly, not looking at her.

"In spite of what I've said to you?" the woman asked.

"What did you say to me?" José asked, still without any inflection in his voice, still without looking at her.

"That business about a million pesos," the woman said.

"I'd already forgotten," José said.

"So do you love me?" the woman asked.

"Yes," said José.

There was a pause. José kept moving about, his face turned toward the cabinets, still not looking at the woman. She blew out another mouthful of smoke, rested her bust on the counter, and then, cautiously and roguishly, biting her tongue before saying it, as if speaking on tiptoe:

"Even if you didn't go to bed with me?" she asked.

And only then did José turn to look at her.

"I love you so much that I wouldn't go to bed with you," he said. Then he walked over to where she was. He stood looking into her face, his powerful arms leaning on the counter in front of her, looking into her eyes. He said: "I love you so much that every night I'd kill the man who goes with you."

At the first instant the woman seemed perplexed. Then she looked at the man attentively, with a wavering expression of compassion and mockery. Then she had a moment of brief disconcerted silence. And then she laughed noisily.

"You're jealous, José. That's wild, you're jealous!"

José blushed again with frank, almost shameful timidity, as might have happened to a child who'd revealed all his secrets all of a sudden. He said:

"This afternoon you don't seem to understand anything, queen." And he wiped himself with the rag. He said:

"This bad life is brutalizing you."

But now the woman had changed her expression.

"So, then," she said. And she looked into his eyes again, with a strange glow in her look, confused and challenging at the same time.

"So you're not jealous."

"In a way I am," José said. "But it's not the way you think."

He loosened his collar and continued wiping himself, drying his throat with the cloth.

"So?" the woman asked.

"The fact is I love you so much that I don't like your doing it," José said.

"What?" the woman asked.

"This business of going with a different man every day," José said.

"Would you really kill him to stop him from going with me?" the woman asked.

"Not to stop him from going with you, no," José said. "I'd kill him because he *went* with you."

"It's the same thing," the woman said.

The conversation had reached an exciting density. The woman was speaking in a soft, low, fascinated voice. Her face was almost stuck up against the man's healthy, peaceful face, as he stood motionless, as if bewitched by the vapor of the words.

"That's true," José said.

"So," the woman said, and reached out her hand to stroke the man's rough arm. With the other she tossed away her butt. "So you're capable of killing a man?"

"For what I told you, yes," José said. And his voice took on an almost dramatic stress.

The woman broke into convulsive laughter, with an obvious mocking intent.

"How awful, José. How awful," she said, still laughing. "José killing a man. Who would have known that behind the fat and sanctimonious man who never makes me pay, who cooks me a steak every day and has fun talking to me until I find a man, there lurks a murderer. How awful, José! You scare me!"

José was confused. Maybe he felt a little indignation. Maybe, when the woman started laughing, he felt defrauded.

"You're drunk, silly," he said. "Go get some sleep. You don't even feel like eating anything."

But the woman had stopped laughing now and was serious again, pensive, leaning on the counter. She watched the man go away. She saw him open the refrigerator and close it again without taking anything out. Then she saw him move to the other end of the counter. She watched him polish the shining glass, the same as in the beginning. Then the woman spoke again with the tender and soft tone of when she said: "Do you really love me, Pepillo?"

"José," she said.

The man didn't look at her.

"José!"

"Go home and sleep," José said. "And take a bath before you go to bed so you can sleep it off."

"Seriously, José," the woman said. "I'm not drunk."

"Then you've turned stupid," José said.

"Come here, I've got to talk to you," the woman said.

The man came over stumbling, halfway between pleasure and mistrust.

"Come closer!"

He stood in front of the woman again. She leaned forward, grabbed him by the hair, but with a gesture of obvious tenderness.

"Tell me again what you said at the start," she said.

"What do you mean?" José asked. He was trying to look at her with his head turned away, held by the hair.

"That you'd kill a man who went to bed with me," the woman said.

"I'd kill a man who went to bed with you, queen. That's right," José said.

The woman let him go.

"In that case you'd defend me if I killed him, right?" she asked affirmatively, pushing José's enormous pig head with a movement of brutal coquettishness. The man didn't answer anything. He smiled.

"Answer me, José," the woman said. "Would you defend me if I killed him?"

"That depends," José said. "You know it's not as easy as you say."

"The police wouldn't believe anyone more than you," the woman said.

José smiled, honored, satisfied. The woman leaned over toward him again, over the counter.

"It's true, José. I'm willing to bet that you've never told a lie in your life," she said.

"You won't get anywhere this way," José said.

"Just the same," the woman said. "The police know you and they'll believe anything without asking you twice."

José began pounding on the counter opposite her, not knowing what to say. The woman looked out at the street again. Then she looked at the clock and modified the tone of her voice, as if she were interested in finishing the conversation before the first customers arrived.

"Would you tell a lie for me, José?" she asked. "Seriously."

And then José looked at her again, sharply, deeply, as if a tremendous idea had come pounding up in his head. An idea that had entered through one ear, spun about for a moment, vague, confused, and gone out through the other, leaving behind only a warm vestige of terror.

"What have you got yourself into, queen?" José asked. He leaned forward, his arms folded over the counter again. The woman caught the strong and ammonia-smelling vapor of his breathing, which had become difficult because of the pressure that the counter was exercising on the man's stomach.

"This is really serious, queen. What have you got yourself into?" he asked.

The woman made her head spin in the opposite direction.

"Nothing," she said. "I was just talking to amuse myself."

Then she looked at him again.

"Do you know you may not have to kill anybody?"

"I never thought about killing anybody," José said, distressed.

"No, man," the woman said. "I mean nobody goes to bed with me."

"Oh!" José said. "Now you're talking straight out. I always thought you had no need to prowl around. I'll make a bet that if you drop all this I'll give you the biggest steak I've got every day, free."

"Thank you, José," the woman said. "But that's not why. It's because I *can't* go to bed with anyone any more."

"You're getting things all confused again," José said. He was becoming impatient.

"I'm not getting anything confused," the woman said. She stretched out on the seat and José saw her flat, sad breasts underneath her brassiere.

"Tomorrow I'm going away and I promise you I won't come back and bother you ever again. I promise you I'll never go to bed with anyone."

"Where'd you pick up that fever?" José asked.

"I decided just a minute ago," the woman said. "Just a minute ago I realized it's a dirty business."

José grabbed the cloth again and started to clean the

glass in front of her. He spoke without looking at her.

He said:

"Of course, the way you do it it's a dirty business. You should have known that a long time ago."

"I was getting to know it a long time ago," the woman said, "but I was only convinced of it just a little while ago. Men disgust me."

José smiled. He raised his head to look at her, still smiling, but he saw her concentrated, perplexed, talking with her shoulders raised, twirling on the stool with a taciturn expression, her face gilded by premature autumnal grain.

"Don't you think they ought to lay off a woman who kills a man because after she's been with him she feels disgust with him and everyone who's been with her?"

"There's no reason to go that far," José said, moved, a thread of pity in his voice.

"What if the woman tells the man he disgusts her while she watches him get dressed because she remembers that she's been rolling around with him all afternoon and feels that neither soap nor sponge can get his smell off her?"

"That all goes away, queen," José said, a little indifferent now, polishing the counter. "There's no reason to kill him. Just let him go."

But the woman kept on talking, and her voice was a uniform, flowing, passionate current.

"But what if the woman tells him he disgusts her and the man stops getting dressed and runs over to her again, kisses her again, does . . .?"

"No decent man would ever do that," José says.

"What if he does?" the woman asks, with exasperating anxiety. "What if the man isn't decent and does it and then the woman feels that he disgusts her so much that she could die, and she knows that the only way to end it all is to stick a knife in under him?"

"That's terrible," José said. "Luckily there's no man who would do what you say."

"Well," the woman said, completely exasperated now. "What if he did? Suppose he did."

"In any case it's not that bad," José said. He kept on cleaning the counter without changing position, less intent on the conversation now.

The woman pounded the counter with her knuckles. She became affirmative, emphatic.

"You're a savage, José," she said. "You don't understand anything." She grabbed him firmly by the sleeve. "Come on, tell me that the woman should kill him."

"O.K.," José said with a conciliatory bias. "It's all probably just the way you say it is."

"Isn't that self-defense?" the woman asked, grabbing him by the sleeve.

Then José gave her a lukewarm and pleasant look.

"Almost, almost," he said. And he winked at her, with an expression that was at the same time a cordial comprehension and a fearful compromise of complicity. But the woman was serious. She let go of him.

"Would you tell a lie to defend a woman who does that?" she asked.

"That depends," said José.

"Depends on what?" the woman asked.

"Depends on the woman," said José.

"Suppose it's a woman you love a lot," the woman said. "Not to be with her, but like you say, you love her a lot."

"O.K., anything you say, queen," José said, relaxed, bored.

He'd gone off again. He'd looked at the clock. He'd seen that it was going on half-past six. He'd thought that in a few minutes the restaurant would be filling up with people and maybe that was why he began to polish the glass with greater effort, looking at the street through the window. The woman stayed on her stool, silent, concentrating, watching the man's movements with an air of declining sadness. Watching him as a lamp about to go out might have looked at a man. Suddenly, without reacting, she spoke again with the unctuous voice of servitude.

"José!"

The man looked at her with a thick, sad tenderness, like a maternal ox. He didn't look at her to hear her, just to look at her, to know that she was there, waiting for a look that had no reason to be one of protection or solidarity. Just the look of a plaything.

"I told you I was leaving tomorrow and you didn't say anything," the woman said.

"Yes," José said. "You didn't tell me where."

"Out there," the woman said. "Where there aren't any men who want to sleep with somebody."

José smiled again.

"Are you really going away?" he asked, as if becoming aware of life, quickly changing the expression on his face.

"That depends on you," the woman said. "If you know enough to say what time I got here, I'll go away tomorrow and I'll never get mixed up in this again. Would you like that?"

José gave an affirmative nod, smiling and concrete. The woman leaned over to where he was.

"If I come back here someday I'll get jealous when I find

another woman talking to you, at this time and on this same stool."

"If you come back here you'll have to bring me something," José said.

"I promise you that I'll look everywhere for the tame bear, bring him to you," the woman said.

José smiled and waved the cloth through the air that separated him from the woman, as if he were cleaning an invisible pane of glass. The woman smiled too, with an expression of cordiality and coquetry now. Then the man went away, polishing the glass to the other end of the counter.

"What, then?" José said without looking at her.

"Will you really tell anyone who asks you that I got here at a quarter to six?" the woman said.

"What for?" José said, still without looking at her now, as if he had barely heard her.

"That doesn't matter," the woman said. "The thing is that you do it."

José then saw the first customer come in through the swinging door and walk over to a corner table. He looked at the clock. It was six-thirty on the dot.

"O.K., queen," he said distractedly. "Anything you say. I always do whatever you want."

"Well," the woman said. "Start cooking my steak, then."

The man went to the refrigerator, took out a plate with a piece of meat on it, and left it on the table. Then he lighted the stove.

"I'm going to cook you a good farewell steak, queen," he said.

"Thank you, Pepillo," the woman said.

She remained thoughtful as if suddenly she had become sunken in a strange subworld peopled with muddy, unknown forms. Across the counter she couldn't hear the noise that the raw meat made when it fell into the burning grease. Afterward she didn't hear the dry and bubbling crackle as José turned the flank over in the frying pan and the succulent smell of the marinated meat by measured moments saturated the air of the restaurant. She remained like that, concentrated, reconcentrated, until she raised her head again, blinking as if she were coming back out of a momentary death. Then she saw the man beside the stove, lighted up by the happy, rising fire.

"Pepillo."

"What!"

"What are you thinking about?" the woman asked.

"I was wondering whether you could find the little wind-up bear someplace," José said.

"Of course I can," the woman said. "But what I want is for you to give me everything I asked for as a going-away present."

José looked at her from the stove.

"How often have I got to tell you?" he said. "Do you want something besides the best steak I've got?"

"Yes," the woman said.

"What is it?" José asked.

"I want another quarter of an hour."

José drew back and looked at the clock. Then he looked at the customer, who was still silent, waiting in the corner, and finally at the meat roasting in the pan. Only then did he speak.

"I really don't understand, queen," he said.

"Don't be foolish, José," the woman said. "Just remember that I've been here since five-thirty."

(1950)

Someone Has Been Disarranging
These Roses

Since it's Sunday and it's stopped raining, I think I'll take a bouquet of roses to my grave. Red and white roses, the kind that she grows to decorate altars and wreaths. The morning has been saddened by the taciturn and overwhelming winter that has set me to remembering the knoll where the townspeople abandon their dead. It's a bare, treeless place, swept only by the providential crumbs that return after the wind has passed. Now that it's stopped raining and the noonday sun has probably hardened the soapy slope, I should be able to reach the grave where my child's body rests, mingled now, dispersed among snails and roots.

She is prostrate before her saints. She's remained abstracted since I stopped moving in the room, when I failed in the first attempt to reach the altar and pick the brightest and freshest roses. Maybe I could have done it today, but the little lamp blinked and she, recovered from her ecstasy, raised her head and looked toward the corner where the chair is. She must have thought: "It's the wind again," because it's true that something creaked beside the altar and the room rocked for an instant, as if the level of the stagnant memories in it for so long had shifted. Then I understood that I would have to wait for another occasion to get the roses because she was still awake, looking at the chair, and she would have heard the sound of my hands beside her face. Now I've got to wait until she leaves the room in a moment and goes to the one next door to sleep her measured and invariable Sunday siesta. Maybe then I can leave with the roses and be back before she returns to this room and remains looking at the chair.

Last Sunday was more difficult. I had to wait almost two hours for her to fall into ecstasy. She seemed restless, preoccupied, as if she had been tormented by the certainty that her solitude in the house had suddenly become less intense. She took several turns about the room with the bouquet of roses before leaving it on the altar. Then she went out into the hallway, turned in, and went to the next room. I knew that she was looking for the lamp. And later, when she passed by the door again and I saw her in the light of the hall with her dark little jacket and her pink stockings, it seemed to me now that she was still the girl who forty years ago had leaned over my bed in that same room and said: "Now that they've put in the toothpicks your eyes are open and hard." She was just the same, as if time hadn't passed since that remote August afternoon when the women brought her into the room and showed her the corpse and told her: "Weep, he was like a brother to you," and she leaned against the wall, weeping, obeying, still soaked from the rain.

For three or four Sundays now I've been trying to get to where the roses are, but she's been vigilant in front of the altar, keeping watch over the roses with a frightened diligence that I hadn't known in her during the twenty years she's been living in the house. Last Sunday, when she went out to get the lamp, I managed to put a bouquet of the best roses together. At no moment had I been closer to fulfilling my desires. But when I was getting ready to return to the chair, I heard her steps in the corridor again. I rearranged the roses on the altar quickly and then I saw her appear in the doorway with the lamp held high.

She was wearing her dark little jacket and the pink stockings, but on her face there was something like the phosphorescence of a revelation. She didn't seem then to be the woman who for twenty years has been growing roses in the garden, but the same child who on that August afternoon had been brought into the next room so that she could change her clothes and who was coming back now with a lamp, fat and grown old, forty years later.

My shoes still have the hard crust of clay that had formed on them that afternoon in spite of the fact that they've been drying beside the extinguished stove for forty years. One day I went to get them. That was after they'd closed up the doors, taken down the bread and the sprig of aloe from the entranceway, and taken away the furniture. All the furniture except for the chair in the corner which has served me as a seat all this time. I knew that the shoes had been set to dry and they didn't even remember them when they abandoned the house. That's why I went to get them.

She returned many years later. So much time had passed that the smell of musk in the room had blended in with the smell of the dust, with the dry and tiny breath of the insects. I was alone in the house, sitting in the corner, waiting. And I had learned to make out the sound of rotting wood, the flutter of the air becoming old in the closed bedrooms. That was when she came. She had stood in the door with a suitcase in her hand, wearing a green hat and the same little cotton jacket that she hadn't taken off ever since then. She was still a girl. She hadn't begun to get fat and her ankles didn't swell under her stockings as they do now. I was covered with dust and cobwebs when she opened the door, and, somewhere in the room, the cricket who'd been singing for twenty years fell silent. But in spite of that, in spite of the cobwebs and the dust, the sudden reluctance of the cricket and the new age of the new arrival, I recognized in her the girl who on that stormy August afternoon had gone with me to collect nests in the stable. Just the way she was, standing in the doorway with the suitcase in her hand and her green hat on, she looked as if she were suddenly going to shout, say the same thing she'd said when they found me face up on the hay-covered stable floor still grasping the railing of the broken stairs. When she opened the door wide the hinges creaked and the dust from the ceiling fell in clumps, as if someone had started hammering on the ridge of the roof, then she paused on the threshold, coming halfway into the room after, and with the voice of someone calling a sleeping person she said: "Boy! Boy!" And I remained still in the chair, rigid, with my feet stretched out.

I thought she had come only to see the room, but she

continued living in the house. She aired out the room and
it was as if she had opened her suitcase and her old smell
of musk had come from it. The others had taken the furniture and clothing away in trunks. She had taken away only
the smells of the room, and twenty years later she brought
them back again, put them in their place, and rebuilt the
little altar, just the way it was before. Her presence alone
was enough to restore what the implacable industry of time
had destroyed. Since then she has eaten and slept in the
room next door, but she spends the day in this one, con-
versing silently with the saints. In the afternoons she sits in
the rocker next to the door and mends clothing. And when
someone comes for a bouquet of roses, she puts the money
in the corner of the kerchief that she ties to her belt and
invariably says: "Pick the ones on the right, those on the left
are for the saints."

That's the way she's been for twenty years, in the rocker,
darning her things, rocking, looking at the chair as if now
she weren't taking care of the boy with whom she had
shared her childhood afternoons but the invalid grandson
who has been sitting here in the corner ever since the time
his grandmother was five years old.

It's possible that now, when she lowers her head again,
I can approach the roses. If I can manage to do so I'll go
to the knoll, lay them on the grave, and come back to my
chair to wait for the day when she won't return to the room
and the sounds will cease in all the rooms.

On that day there'll be a change in all this, because I'll
have to leave the house again in order to tell someone that
the rose woman, the one who lives in the tumble-down
house, is in need of four men to take her to the knoll. Then

I'll be alone forever in the room. But, on the other hand, she'll be satisfied. Because on that day she'll learn that it wasn't the invisible wind that came to her altar every Sunday and disarranged the roses.

(1952)

The Night of the Curlews

We WERE SITTING, the three of us, around the table, when someone put a coin in the slot and the Wurlitzer played once more the record that had been going all night. The rest happened so fast that we didn't have time to think. It happened before we could remember where we were, before we could get back our sense of location. One of us reached his hand out over the counter, groping (we couldn't see the hand, we heard it), bumped into a glass, and then was still, with both hands resting on the hard surface. Then the three of us looked for ourselves in the darkness and found ourselves there, in the joints of the thirty fingers piled up on the counter. One of us said:

"Let's go."

And we stood up as if nothing had happened. We still hadn't had time to get upset.

In the hallway, as we passed, we heard the nearby music spinning out at us. We caught the smell of sad women sitting and waiting. We felt the prolonged emptiness of the hall before us while we walked toward the door, before the other smell came out to greet us, the sour smell of the woman sitting by the door. We said:

"We're leaving."

The woman didn't answer anything. We heard the creak of a rocking chair, rising up as she stood. We heard the footsteps on the loose board and the return of the woman again, when the hinges creaked once more and the door closed behind us.

We turned around. Right there, behind us, there was a harsh, cutting breeze of an invisible dawn, and a voice that said:

"Get out of the way, I'm coming through with this."

We moved back. And the voice spoke again:

"You're still against the door."

And only then, when we'd moved to all sides and had found the voice everywhere, did we say:

"We can't get out of here. The curlews have pecked out our eyes."

Then we heard several doors open. One of us let go of the other hands and we heard him dragging along in the darkness, weaving, bumping into the things that surrounded us. He spoke from somewhere in the darkness.

"We must be close," he said. "There's a smell of piled-up trunks around here."

We felt the contact of his hands again. We leaned against

the wall and another voice passed by then, but in the opposite direction.

"They might be coffins," one of us said.

The one who had dragged himself into the corner and
was breathing beside us now said:

"They're trunks. Ever since I was little I've been able to
tell the smell of stored clothing."

Then we moved in that direction. The ground was soft
and smooth, fine earth that had been walked on. Someone
held out a hand. We felt the contact with long, live skin, but
we no longer felt the wall opposite.

"This is a woman," we said.

The other one, the one who had spoken of trunks, said:

"I think she's asleep."

The body shook under our hands, trembled, we felt it
slip away, not as if it had got out of our reach, but as if it
had ceased to exist. Still, after an instant in which we remained motionless, stiffened, leaning against each other's
shoulders, we heard her voice.

"Who's there?" it said.

"It's us," we replied without moving.

The movement of the bed could be heard, the creaking
and the shuffling of feet looking for slippers in the darkness. Then we pictured the seated woman, looking at us as
when she still hadn't awakened completely.

"What are you doing here?" she asked.

And we answered:

"We don't know. The curlews pecked out our eyes."

The voice said that she'd heard something about that.
That the newspapers had said that three men had been
drinking in a courtyard where there were five or six curlews.

Seven curlews. One of the men began singing like a curlew, imitating them.

"The worst was that he was an hour behind," she said. "That was when the birds jumped on the table and pecked out their eyes."

She said that's what the newspapers had said, but nobody had believed them. We said:

"If people had gone there, they'd have seen the curlews."

And the woman said:

"They did. The courtyard was full of people the next day, but the woman had already taken the curlews somewhere else."

When he turned around, the woman stopped speaking. There was the wall again. By just turning around we would find the wall. Around us, surrounding us, there was always a wall. One let go of our hands again. We heard him crawling again, smelling the ground, saying:

"Now I don't know where the trunks are. I think we're somewhere else now."

And we said:

"Come here. Somebody's here next to us."

We heard him come close. We felt him stand up beside us and again his warm breath hit us in the face.

"Reach out that way," we told him. "There's someone we know there."

He must have reached out, he must have moved toward the place we indicated, because an instant later he came back to tell us:

"I think it's a boy."

And we told him:

"Fine. Ask him if he knows us."

He asked the question. We heard the apathetic and simple voice of the boy, who said:

"Yes, I know you. You're the three men whose eyes were pecked out by the curlews."

Then an adult voice spoke. The voice of a woman who seemed to be behind a closed door, saying:

"You're talking to yourself again."

And the child's voice, unconcerned, said:

"No. The men who had their eyes pecked out by the curlews are here again."

There was a sound of hinges and then the adult voice, closer than the first time.

"Take them home," she said.

And the boy said:

"I don't know where they live."

And the adult voice said:

"Don't be mean. Everybody knows where they live ever since the night the curlews pecked their eyes out."

Then she went on in a different tone, as if she were speaking to us:

"What happened is that nobody wanted to believe it and they say it was a fake item made up by the papers to boost their circulation. No one has seen the curlews."

And he said:

"But nobody would believe me if I led them along the street."

We didn't move. We were still, leaning against the wall, listening to her. And the woman said:

"If this one wants to take you it's different. After all, nobody would pay much attention to what a boy says."

The child's voice cut in:

"If I go out onto the street with them and say that they're

the men who had their eyes pecked out by the curlews, the boys will throw stones at me. Everybody on the street says it couldn't have happened."

There was a moment of silence. Then the door closed again and the boy spoke:

"Besides, I'm reading *Terry and the Pirates* right now."

Someone said in our ear:

"I'll convince him."

He crawled over to where the voice was.

"I like it," he said. "At least tell us what happened to Terry this week."

He's trying to gain his confidence, we thought. But the boy said:

"That doesn't interest me. The only thing I like are the colors."

"Terry's in a maze," we said.

And the boy said:

"That was Friday. Today's Sunday and what I like are the colors," and he said it with a cold, dispassionate, indifferent voice.

When the other one came back, we said:

"We've been lost for almost three days and we haven't had a moment's rest."

And one said:

"All right. Let's rest awhile, but without letting go of each other's hands."

We sat down. An invisible sun began to warm us on the shoulders. But not even the presence of the sun interested us. We felt it there, everywhere, having already lost the notion of distance, time, direction. Several voices passed.

"The curlews pecked out our eyes," we said.

And one of the voices said:

"These here took the newspapers seriously."

The voices disappeared. And we kept on sitting, like that, shoulder to shoulder, waiting, in that passing of voices, in that passing of images, for a smell or a voice that was known to us to pass. The sun was above our heads, still warming us. Then someone said:

"Let's go toward the wall again."

And the others, motionless, their heads lifted toward the invisible light:

"Not yet. Let's just wait till the sun begins to burn us on the face."

(1953)